Safe in the Tycoon's Arms

—

Jennifer Faye

D0838263

H HARLEQUIN® ROMANCE

Recycling programs
for this product may
not exist in your area.

ISBN-13: 978-0-373-74282-0

SAFE IN THE TYCOON'S ARMS

First North American Publication 2014

Printed in U.S.A.

HARLEQUIN®
www.Harlequin.com

In another life **Jennifer Faye** was a statistician. She still has a love for numbers, formulas and spreadsheets, but when she was presented with the opportunity to follow her lifelong passion and spend her days writing and pursuing her dream of becoming a Harlequin® author, she couldn't pass it up. These days, when she's not writing, Jennifer enjoys reading, fine needlework, quilting, tweeting and cheering on the Pittsburgh Penguins. She lives in Pennsylvania with her amazingly patient husband, two remarkably talented daughters and their two very spoiled fur babies, otherwise known as cats—but *shh*...don't tell them they're not human!

Jennifer loves to hear from readers—you can contact her via her website, www.jenniferfaye.com.

Recent books by Jennifer Faye

SNOWBOUND WITH THE SOLDIER
RANCHER TO THE RESCUE

These and other titles by Jennifer Faye are available in ebook format from www.Harlequin.com

For Viv.

Thank you for being such a good friend over the years. Your helpful advice and unending support are deeply appreciated. Here's to the future of possibilities.

CHAPTER ONE

A DEAFENING CRACK of thunder rumbled through the darkened house. Kate Whitley pressed a hand to her pounding chest. She'd hated storms since she was a little kid. A brilliant flash of lightning sent shards of light slashing across the hallway while rain pelted the window.

Mother Nature certainly had a wicked sense of humor. Actually, it seemed as though life as a whole was mocking Kate. Absolutely nothing was going according to plan, no matter how hard she fought to put things right.

Her fingers pushed against the cold metallic plate on the swinging hall door. Inside the kitchen, the glare from the overhead light caused her to squint. What in the world was going on? She could have sworn she'd turned everything off before going upstairs. Hadn't she?

She sighed and shook her head. Her mind must be playing tricks on her. The long nights of tossing and turning instead of sleeping were finally catching up to her. And it couldn't have happened at a worse time. In a few more hours, she had to be fully alert. There were decisions only she could make—lifesaving decisions.

If only she could get a little shut-eye, she'd be able to think clearly. But first, Mother Nature had to quiet down. No one could rest with all this ruckus.

It didn't ease her nerves being away from home, even if she was staying in a New York City mansion. This place was nothing like her two-bedroom, ranch-style house in Pennsylvania. Though this oversize house contained some of the most breathtaking architecture, there was something missing—the warmth that made a building more than just a place to hang your coat, the coziness that made it home.

In a big city where she barely knew anyone, she and this house had a couple of things in common—being lonely and forgotten. Somehow it seemed like fate that she'd ended up in this deserted mansion. A warm, loving home had somehow always eluded her, and just when she thought she'd made one of her own, it too was about to be snatched out from under her.

Sadness weighed heavily on her as her bare feet moved silently across the kitchen tiles. The coldness raced up through her pink painted toes to her bare legs and sent goose bumps cascading down her arms. Spring may have brought warmer days, but the nights were still chilly. She rubbed her palms up and down her arms, willing away her discomfort. Perhaps her long T-shirt wasn't the warmest choice for this soggy night, but with her living out of a suitcase, her choices were quite limited.

She yawned and opened the door of the stainless-steel refrigerator. She hadn't had any appetite until now. With so much riding on this upcoming meeting, she'd ended up with a stress headache for most of the day. But back here ensconced between these quiet, peaceful walls, the pain had loosened its vicelike grip.

Now she needed something to ease her hunger pangs. Other than a few meager groceries she'd placed in there earlier, the glass shelves were bare. The friend who'd let her stay here free of charge said the owner was out of town and wouldn't be back anytime soon. From the empty cabinets to the dust-covered bedrooms, Kate deduced no one had lived here in quite a while.

With an apple in hand, she filled a glass of water. She'd just turned off the faucet when she heard faint but distinct footsteps. The hairs on the back of her neck rose. Either this place had some mighty big rats…or she wasn't alone.

"Stop right there!" boomed a male voice.

So much for the rat theory.

Her heart lodged in her throat, blocking a terrified scream. Who was this man? And what did he want with her? Her lungs started to burn. Was he a thief, a desperate junkie…or worse?

She struggled to suck air past the enormous lump in her throat. A nervous tremor in her hand caused droplets of water to spill over the rim of the glass. Why had she put herself in such peril by making the rash decision to stay in this deserted house alone? After all, what did she know about her newfound friend? Not much. They'd only met a week ago. The older woman had seemed so nice—so understanding in Kate's time of need.

She wondered if a scream would carry to any of the neighboring houses on the block. Probably not. This house came from an era when structures were built with thick, sturdy walls. She was on her own.

"You shouldn't be here." She fought to keep her voice steady. "This place has a burglar alarm. It won't be long until the police show up. I haven't seen your face. You can escape out the back and I won't tell anyone."

"I don't think so. Turn around."

Not about to let this stranger know how much he frightened her, she placed the glass on the counter, leveled her shoulders and took an unsteady breath. When she went to turn, her feet wouldn't move. They were stuck to the floor as though weighted down in concrete.

A crescendo of thunder reverberated through her body. The house plunged into darkness. Kate bit down on her bottom lip to keep a frightened gasp bottled up.

Don't panic. Stay calm.

Could this really be happening? What had she done to piss off Fate and have it turn on her? Hysterical laughter swelled in her throat. With effort, she choked it down. It wouldn't help anything for this man to think she was losing it.

Drawing on every bit of courage she could muster, she forced her feet to move. Once fully turned around, she squinted into the dark shadows but could only make out the man's vague outline. Who was he? What did he want with her?

Then, as though in answer to her prayer, the power blinked back on. When her vision adjusted, she found herself staring at a bare male chest. *What in the world?* Her wide-eyed gaze dropped farther past his trim waist but screeched to a halt upon the discovery of this stranger's only article of clothing—navy boxer shorts.

This night was definitely getting stranger by the second.

She couldn't resist a second glance at her sexy intruder. He definitely wasn't a kid, having filled out in all the right places. She'd only ever seen defined muscles like his in the glossy pages of magazines, and this guy would qualify with his washboard abs. He must be around her age, maybe a little older.

When her gaze rose up over his six feet plus of sexiness, she met a hard glint in his blue-gray eyes. He obviously wasn't any happier about discovering her than she was of stumbling across him.

"What are you doing here?" The stranger's deep voice held a note of authority as though he were used to commanding people's attention.

"Wondering why you're standing in my kitchen."

The frown lines on his face etched even deeper. "This is your place?"

Technically no, but she wasn't about to explain her unusual circumstances to Mr. Oh-So-Sexy. She merely nodded, affirming her right to be there.

His brow arched in disbelief.

Who was he to pass judgment? When she pressed her hands to her hips, she realized he wasn't the only one scantily dressed. With the hem of her worn but comfy shirt pinched between her fingers, she pulled it down as far as the material would allow. Instinct told her to run and put on something more modest. But in order to do that, she'd have to cross his path. Not a great idea.

Her gaze strayed back to the doorway. Sooner or later she'd have to make her move. She wanted to believe he wasn't there to hurt her—wanted to accept the notion that there was some crazy explanation for the nearly naked man standing in front of her, but her mind drew a blank. She glanced back at him, taking in his blondish-brown wavy hair tousled as though he'd just woken up. And his lack of apparel left no room for doubt that he was unarmed.

"Don't look so panicked. I have no intention of hurting you." His deep voice was as smooth and rich as hot fudge. "I just want some answers."

She stuck out her chin. "That makes two of us."

"I guess you should start explaining." He looked at her expectantly.

Kate crossed her arms. He wasn't going to boss her around. She had every right to be here. Then an ominous thought came to her: Who was to say Connie hadn't made a similar offer to this man? But wouldn't it have crossed her friend's mind that this would create an awkward situation to have two strangers—a man and a woman—alone in the house?

As she kept a wary eye on him, she noticed something familiar about him. The thought niggled at her. She couldn't put her finger on where she'd seen him before, probably because the only thing keeping her on her feet right now was adrenaline. She needed sleep. Desperately. But how would she get this man to put on some clothes and go away?

"No more stalling." Lucas Carrington's patience was worn razor thin. Tired of talking in circles, he cut to the chase. "Who are you? And what are you doing here?"

Her lush lips pursed as her eyes narrowed. "My name is Kate Whitley and I have every right to be here—"

"Impossible. More likely you're homeless and broke in here seeking shelter from the storm."

Kate's chin tilted up and her unwavering brown gaze met his. "I'm not homeless. In fact, I'm an interior designer and a darned good one, too."

She did have an innocent girl-next-door look about her, but he knew all too well that things were never quite what they seemed. "Are you trying to tell me you broke in here because you had this overwhelming desire to redecorate the place?"

Her thin shoulders drew back into a firm line. Her threadbare cartoon T-shirt pulled snugly across her pert breasts. He swallowed hard. Okay, so maybe his first assessment of her hadn't been quite right. Gorgeous. Sexy. Curvaceous. Those were much more fitting descriptions.

She continued to glare at him, seemingly oblivious to the fact her demeanor was more alluring than intimidating. And like some hormone-fueled teenager, he found himself unable to turn away from her tempting curves.

"There's no need to sound so condescending." Her voice filled with exasperation.

With effort, his gaze lifted to meet hers. "I'm calling the police. They can deal with you." But there was a wrinkle in his plan—his cell phone was in the other room and the landline in the kitchen had been disconnected ages ago.

"Go right ahead."

Her confident tone surprised him. Did she expect her beauty to get her out of this mess? Or was she attempting to pull a con job on him? Not that any of it mattered. He didn't have a problem calling her bluff.

"You seem fairly certain you won't get in trouble—"

"I won't."

Lucas was having a hard time focusing on the conversation given that his unexpected visitor was standing in his kitchen with nothing on but a T-shirt, which clung to her shapely curves and exposed her long, long legs. He was definitely beginning to understand why she might rely on her looks. And if he kept staring, this could get embarrassing for both of them.

He forced his gaze to her face, not that it was

any less distracting. Was she wearing makeup? Or was her skin naturally that smooth and creamy?

Even more troubling than how beautiful he found her was the way she reminded him too much of the past—a past that had nearly destroyed him. Not so long ago another beautiful woman had stood in that spot. She'd made him promises but ended up breaking each and every one of them. His jaw tightened. The last thing he needed was this stranger's presence to dredge up memories he'd fought so hard to seal inside. He refused to let it happen.

Refocused and clear about his priorities, his gaze returned to her warm brown eyes. She stared directly at him. Pink stained her cheeks, but she didn't glance away. She stepped forward, using the kitchen island as a shield. It was far too late for modesty. Her sexy form was already emblazoned upon his memory.

Stay focused. Soon she'll be gone. One way... or the other.

He cleared his throat. "Okay, you've got my attention. Why won't you get in trouble?"

"I have permission to be here. Temporarily, that is. You know, while the owner is out of town." Kate's eyes narrowed, challenging him. She certainly was confident. He'd give her that. "And now it's your turn to do some explaining. Who are you?"

"My name's Lucas."

"Well, Lucas, I assume you must know Connie, too."

His gaze sought out hers and held it. "Connie? Is that who let you in here?"

Kate nodded as hope sparked in her eyes. "Connie Carrington."

He had liked it better when he thought Kate was a squatter looking for a warm place to sleep. "To be sure, describe Connie."

"Short. Brunette. Sixtyish. Very sweet and generous. She has a friendly smile and volunteers at East Riverview Hospital."

"That's her." It still didn't prove Kate was telling the whole truth, but it was sure looking that way.

"Here's the thing, Connie obviously offered me this place first. And I don't think us sharing the house is going to work."

How dare this woman—this stranger—kick him out of his own house? He opened his mouth to give her a piece of his mind but then closed it. Obviously she didn't recognize him, a small wonder after that ridiculous magazine article earlier in the month had named him Bachelor of the Year. His quiet life hadn't been the same since then.

Kate was a refreshing change from the headline seekers and the husband hunters. Maybe if this were a different time under different circumstances, he'd welcome this beautiful intrusion. But right now all he wanted was to be left alone.

A clap of thunder rattled the windows. Kate jumped. She obviously wasn't as calm as she'd like him to believe. Perhaps they both needed a moment to gather their thoughts. He certainly could use a minute or two to tamp down his unwanted attraction.

"This conversation would be a little less awkward with some more clothes on. I'll be right back." He started out of the room, then as an afterthought he called over his shoulder, "Don't go anywhere."

Lucas strode from the room. His teeth ground together. He didn't want this woman here. He never had company and he preferred it that way. In fact, the less time he spent here, the better he liked it. When he'd asked his aunt to look after the place, he'd never expected her to turn it into a B and B. What in the world had she been thinking?

Maybe his aunt had planned for him to never find out about Kate. After all, he wasn't even supposed to be home for another week. But one untimely setback after another at the future site of Carrington Gems' expansion in San Francisco had ground construction to a halt.

Still, it was more than losing money hand over fist due to bureaucratic red tape that had him cutting his trip short. He put a stop to his thoughts.

He wasn't ready to contemplate the devastating situation he'd faced before catching his cross-country flight home.

And the last thing he needed was to return home to find a half-dressed woman making herself comfortable in his house. The image of her bare legs teased his mind, clouding his thoughts.

He cursed under his breath and pulled on the first pair of jeans he laid his hands on. But if he was going to stay focused, his beautiful interloper needed to cover up. He grabbed a heavy robe that should modestly cover her and give him some peace of mind. With a T-shirt in hand for himself, he rushed back to the kitchen clutching both articles of clothing.

"Here." He held out the robe to her. "Put this on."

Her wary gaze moved to his outstretched hand and back. It was then that he got a close-up view of her heart-shaped face and button nose. His thoughts screeched to a halt when he spied the dark shadows beneath her eyes. Sympathy welled up inside his chest. Not so long ago, he'd worn a similar look. It hadn't happened by missing a night or two of sleep. In fact, it'd been the worst time of his life. His gut told him that Kate had a devastating story of her own.

He'd always been good at reading people. It was what helped him run Carrington Gems and hire a reliable staff. So why had he immediately jumped to the wrong conclusion about Kate?

Had his experience with his ex-wife jaded him so badly that he wasn't even willing to give this woman the benefit of the doubt? Or was it the fact she was standing in this house—a place so filled with pain and loss?

Kate's cold fingertips brushed over the back of his hand as she accepted the robe. His instinct was to take her hands in his and rub them until they were warm. But he resisted the temptation. She wasn't his guest…his responsibility.

While she slipped on the robe, he stepped back, giving her some space. He pulled the shirt over his head. Now they could have a reasonable conversation.

Fully clothed, he glanced up, finding Kate's brows furrowed as she stared at him. He followed her line of vision to a large hole in his jeans above his knee as well as the army of white smudges marking up both legs. He really should consider tossing them, but they were just so comfortable. Wait. Why should he care what this woman thought of him or his clothes? After tonight he'd never see her again.

Kate shoved up the sleeves on the robe and crossed her arms. "What do you propose we do?"

In any other situation, he'd show her to the door and wish her well. After all, she wasn't his problem. And being drawn in by her very kissable lips and the memory of how that threadbare shirt hugged her curves was a complication in his life that he just didn't need.

But her pale face with those dark smudges beneath her eyes dug at his resolve.

And he couldn't dismiss the fact his aunt had sent Kate to stay here. Not that his aunt didn't help people on a daily basis, but she knew this house was off-limits to everyone. That meant Kate was someone special. Now he really needed to speak to his aunt, but first he had to make things clear to Kate.

"There's something you should know. This is my house."

CHAPTER TWO

KATE EYED UP Mr. Oh-So-Sexy's faded T-shirt and threadbare denim. Even her ratty old jeans were in better condition. Did she look gullible enough to swallow his story that he was the owner of this mansion? That would make him wealthy. Very wealthy. And he sure didn't look the part.

"Why should I believe you own this house?"

He frowned. "Because I'm Lucas Carrington. Connie's nephew."

His unwavering tone gave her pause. She studied his aristocratic nose, piercing blue eyes and sensual lips. The wheels in her mind began to spin. No wonder he seemed so familiar. During her many hours at the hospital, she'd ended up thumbing through one magazine after the other. It was within one of those stylish periodicals that she'd skimmed over an article listing this year's most eligible bachelors.

Lucas Carrington had been named Bachelor of the Year. And he had been by far the steamiest candidate on the list. And that had been before she'd garnered a glimpse of his ripped abs. Her mouth grew dry at the memory. She instantly squashed the thought.

The reality of the situation at last sunk in. That man—the hunk from the popular magazine—was standing in front of her in his bare feet. And she was accusing him of being an intruder. This had to be some sort of crazy, mixed-up dream.

"I see my name has rung a bell." Smugness reflected in his captivating eyes. "Perhaps my aunt mentioned me."

The fact he'd been holding that ace up his sleeve the whole time instead of introducing himself up front annoyed her. She wasn't about to fold her hand so quickly—even if she had been beaten already.

She conjured up her best poker face. "Actually, Connie went to great pains not to mention you. She merely said the owner was out of town for an extended period. In fact, when I saw the condition of this place, I didn't think anyone had lived here in years."

A muscle twitched in his cheek as his gaze moved away. "I only need a couple of the rooms. Even when I'm in town, I'm not here much."

"I see." What else could she say? That it was a bit strange to live in a mansion filled with cobwebs and covered in a blanket of dust? But who was she to judge? She was living out of a suitcase, and by the end of the month, she would be technically homeless. The thought of being adrift with no place to call home sent her stomach plummeting. But she could only deal with one problem at a time.

Lucas shifted uncomfortably. "Why do you keep looking at me strangely?"

"I'm trying to decide whether I should believe you. I mean, I wouldn't expect such a wealthy man to wear…umm, that." She pointed at his tattered jeans.

Even though she knew that he was in fact Lucas Carrington, she didn't want to let on just yet. After all, he hadn't readily taken her word that she wasn't a squatter. Why not let him see what it was like not to be believed?

He shrugged. "So they're old jeans. It doesn't mean anything."

"I don't know. This could all be an act. How am I to know that you aren't pretending to be the owner? Maybe I should call the police and let them sort this out."

Instead of the angry response she'd been anticipating, the corners of his mouth lifted. Was that a smile? Her stomach somersaulted.

"I guess I deserve that. Wait here." He set off in the same direction he'd gone to grab his clothes and the robe he'd loaned her.

The scorching hot image of him in those boxer shorts flashed in her mind. Her pulse kicked up a notch or two. If Lucas wasn't already wealthy, he could make a fortune as an underwear model. She'd be first in line to buy the magazine.

Still a bit chilled, she snuggled up in the robe, noticing the fresh scent of aftershave. She lifted the plush material to her nose, unable to resist inhaling even deeper. *Mmm...*

"Is the robe okay?" His smooth, deep voice filled the room.

"Umm...yes." She smoothed the lapel. "I was just admiring its...its softness."

He nodded, but she wondered if he'd caught her getting high off his very masculine scent. No man had a right to smell that good or look that hot with his clothes on...or off.

He skirted around the kitchen island and headed for her. Kate held her ground, all the while wondering what he was up to.

"Here." He flipped open a black wallet. "This should clear things up."

Her fingers slid across the worn smooth leather. She really didn't need to see his driver's license, but she had started this, so she might as well follow through.

She glanced at the photo of a neatly groomed man in a suit and tie. Definitely Lucas, but the spiffed-up version. The funny thing was she liked him in his worn-out jeans and sloppy T-shirt as much if not more than his business persona.

"So now do you believe me?" he asked with a tone of smug satisfaction, as if he'd just one-upped her.

She didn't like him thinking that he'd gotten the best of her.

"I don't know." She held the ID up beside his face, hmm-ing and hah-ing, as though trying to make up her mind. "There's definitely a resemblance, but I'm not sure."

He yanked the card from her hand and stared at it. "Of course it's me! And that's my address… this address."

At last he'd fallen off his cool, confident edge. A smile pulled at her lips. The action felt so foreign to her after the past few stressful months, but the lightness grew, erupting into laughter. The more she laughed, the deeper Lucas frowned. It had been so long since she'd had an occasion to laugh that she didn't want it to end. It felt so good. So liberating. So freeing.

His brow arched. "Have I amused you enough?"

Her cheeks started to ache and she forced herself to calm down. After dabbing both eyes, she gazed up at him. "Sorry about that. But you don't know how much I needed that laugh."

His brows rose higher, but he didn't ask why and it was just as well. She wasn't about to spill her sorrowful tale to this stranger. In fact, she suddenly felt guilty for her outburst. Not because it was at Lucas's expense. He was a big boy who could take a little ribbing. It was the thought of her little girl in the hospital that sobered her mood. Under the circumstances, Kate had no right to smile, much less laugh.

If the hospital staff hadn't invoked their stupid policy, she'd still be there—sitting by Molly's bed or haunting the halls. But the nurses had insisted she needed some rest so she didn't wear herself out.

"Hey, what's the matter?" Lucas stepped closer. His hand reached out as though to touch Kate's shoulder, but then he hesitated.

She blinked back the rush of emotions. "I'm fine. I'll just get my things and get out of your way."

His hand lowered to his side as he glanced around the room. "Where exactly are your things?"

"Upstairs."

"But those rooms aren't fit for anyone. I dismissed the maid service as soon as… It doesn't matter. The only important thing is keeping you out of that mess."

"It isn't so dirty now." At the shocked look on Lucas's face, she continued. "Or at least the room that I'm staying in is mostly clean."

"What room?" His face creased with worry lines.

A crack of thunder sounded, followed by the lights flickering. Kate wrapped her arms around herself. "The one at the end of the hall."

His shoulders drew back in a rigid line as his brows gathered in a dark, intimidating line. "Which end?"

Kate pointed straight overhead.

His shoulders drooped as he let out a sigh. "What in the world was my aunt thinking to send you here?"

Kate had wondered the exact same thing, but she'd come to the conclusion that Connie had only the best intentions…even if they were a little misguided. Now it was time to move on.

Lucas watched as Kate snuggled deeper in his robe. A resigned look etched across her weary features as the dark circles made her eyes appear much too large for her face. She reminded him of a puppy who'd been kicked to the curb and forgotten.

His thoughts rolled back in time to the day when he'd found a stray pup and brought it home. Everyone but his aunt had told him to get rid of the filthy beast. Aunt Connie had been different. She could see what the others couldn't be bothered to look at—the puppy's need to be loved and cared for. More than that she recognized Lucas's need for something calming in the upheaval that was his life.

Lucas brought his thoughts up short. Kate wasn't a stray puppy. She was a grown woman who could care for herself. He had enough problems. He didn't need to be embroiled in someone else's. He should wish her well and be done with it.

A loud boom of thunder shook the very floor they stood on. Kate wrapped her arms around herself as her wide eyes turned toward the window. This storm was showing no signs of letting up. Definitely not a night to be out and about.

If only he knew why his aunt had sent her here....

Kate turned and started down the hall.

"Wait." Unease mounted within him as he realized what he was about to do.

"For what?" Kate asked, stepping back into the kitchen.

He noticed how the rest of her short dark brown hair was tucked behind each ear as though she'd been too busy to worry about what she looked like. The concept of a woman going out in public without taking great pains with her appearance was new to him. This mystery woman intrigued him and that was not good—not good at all.

But more than that, he'd witnessed how every

time it thundered, she jumped and the fear reflected in her eyes. He couldn't turn her out into the stormy night—especially when he suspected she had nowhere else to go.

Going against his better judgment, he said, "You don't have to leave tonight."

"Yes, I do."

"Would you quit being so difficult?"

She glowered at him. "But you just got done telling me that you wanted me out of here right away. You're the one being difficult."

He inwardly groaned with frustration. "That was before. Give me a moment to speak with my aunt."

"I don't see how that will change anything. Unless you're still worried that I'm a liar and a thief."

"That isn't what I meant." He jerked his fingers through his hair. "Just wait here for a minute, okay? In fact, sit down. You look dead on your feet."

Her eyes narrowed. Her pale lips drooped into a frown. He'd obviously said the wrong thing... again, but darned if he knew what had upset her. Maybe it was mentioning how tired she looked. In his limited experience with women, they never wanted to look anything less than amazing, no matter the circumstances.

When Kate didn't move, he walked over and

pulled out a chair at the table. "Please sit down. I won't be long."

He stepped inside the small bedroom just off the kitchen, which at one point in the house's history had been the domestic help's quarters. Lucas now claimed it as his bedroom—not that he spent much time there. His cell phone was sitting on the nightstand next to the twin bed.

He selected his aunt's name from his frequently called list. His fingers tightened around the phone as he held it to his ear. After only one ring, it switched to voice mail.

"Call me as soon as you get this." His voice was short and clipped.

He couldn't help but wonder where she might be and why she wasn't taking his call. Would she still be at the hospital doing her volunteer work? He glanced at the alarm clock. At this late hour, he highly doubted it.

With his aunt unaccounted for, he'd have to follow his gut. He'd already determined Kate wasn't a criminal. But what would he do with her? Sit and hash out what was bothering her to see if he could help? Certainly not.

He rubbed his hand over his stubbled jaw. He didn't want to get pulled any further into her problems. No matter what her circumstances were, it had nothing to do with him. Come tomorrow, she'd have to find other accommodations.

Still uncomfortable with his decision, he stepped back into the kitchen. Kate was seated at the table. Her arms were crossed on the glass tabletop, cradling her head. He must have made a sound, because she jerked upright in her seat.

Kate blinked before stretching. "Did Connie confirm what I told you?"

"Actually she didn't—"

"What? But I'm not lying."

"No one said you were. But my aunt isn't available. So how about we make a deal?"

A yawn escaped her lips. "What do you have in mind?"

"I'll give you the benefit of the doubt, if you'll do the same for me."

Kate was quiet for a moment as though weighing his words. "I suppose. But what does it matter now?"

"Because you and I are going to be housemates for the night."

"What? But I couldn't—"

"Yes, you can. Have you looked outside lately? It's pouring. And it's late at night."

Her lips pressed into a firm line as she got to her feet and pushed in the chair. "I don't need your charity."

"Who says it's charity? You'd be saving me from a load of trouble with my aunt if she found out I kicked you to the curb on a night like this."

Kate's hand pressed to her hip, which was hidden beneath the folds of the oversize robe. "Are you being on the level?"

She didn't have any idea what it was costing him to ask her to stay, even for one night. This place was a tomb of memories. He didn't want anyone inside here, witnessing his utter failure to keep his family together.

But there was something special about her—more than the way that he was thoroughly drawn to her. There was a vulnerability in her gaze. Something he'd guess she'd gone to great pains to hide from everyone, but he'd noticed. Maybe because he'd been vulnerable before, too.

"You don't look too sure about this."

He was usually much better at hiding his thoughts, but the dismal events of the day combined with the lateness of the hour were his undoing.

"I'm not. Let's just go to bed." Her drooping eyelids lifted and he immediately realized how his words could be misconstrued. "Alone."

CHAPTER THREE

THE SUN HAD yet to flirt with the horizon when Kate awoke to the alarm on her cell phone. Though she'd only snuck in a few hours of sleep, she felt refreshed. Her heart was full of hope that today her most fervent prayer would be answered.

It will all work out. It has to.

As she rushed through the shower, the what-ifs and maybes started to crowd into her mind. Finding a cure to her daughter's brain tumor had been rife with negative diagnoses. That was why they were here in New York City—to see a surgeon who was willing to do the seemingly impossible. But what if—

Don't go there. Not today.

With her resolve to think only positive thoughts, she pulled on a red skirt and a white top from her suitcase. The light tap of the continued rain on the window reminded her of the night before and meeting Lucas Carrington. He definitely presented a distraction from her attack of nerves. She wondered if he'd be just as devastatingly handsome in the daylight. She tried to convince herself that it'd been the exhaustion talking, that no man could look that good. But she'd seen the magazine spread with him shaved and spruced up in a tux. He really was that good-looking. Which raised the question: What was he doing living here in this unkempt, mausoleumlike house?

Kate proceeded down the grand staircase, with her suitcase in one hand and her purse in the other. She hated the fact that she would never learn the history or secrets of this mansion. This would be her last trip down the cinematic steps. She paused to take one last look around.

She was in awe of the house's old-world grandeur. Her gaze skimmed over the cream paint and paused to inspect the various paintings adorning the walls. Her nose curled up. She knew a bit about art from her work as an interior designer and these modern pieces, though not to her liking, would still fetch a hefty chunk of change at auction.

Even though the current decor didn't match the home's old-world elegance, she still saw the beauty lurking in the background. In her experience, she'd never found such charm and detailed work in any of the newer structures. Sure, they were all beautiful in their own unique ways, but this mansion was brimming with personality that only time could provide. She'd be willing to bet that if the walls could talk they'd spin quite a tale. She was certain that given the opportunity to rejuvenate this place, she could learn a considerable amount about its history. But she'd never have that chance.

With a resigned sigh, she set her suitcase by the front door before heading back the hall to the kitchen. She couldn't shake the dismal thought of Lucas turning a blind eye to the house's disintegrating state and letting the place fall into utter disrepair. Who could do such a thing? Was it possible he didn't realize the real damage being done by his neglect?

If the man took the time to walk upstairs once in a while, he'd notice the work that needed to be done. Some of the repairs were blatantly obvious. It was a little hard to miss the *drip-drip-drip* last night as the rain leaked through the ceiling of her bedroom. She'd used a waste basket to collect the water. Maybe she should say something…

No. Don't go there. This house and Lucas are absolutely none of your business.

She paused outside the kitchen door and listened. No sounds came from within. She wasn't so sure she was up to facing him in the light of day after getting caught last night in her nightshirt. Still she refused to just slip away without thanking him for his generosity.

She pushed the door open and tiptoed into the room, hoping not to disturb him since his bedroom was just off the kitchen. Now if only she knew where to find a pen and some paper to write a note.

"You're up early."

Kate jumped. It took a second for her heart to sink back into her chest. She turned to find Mr. Oh-So-Sexy sitting off to the side in the breakfast nook with the morning paper and a cup of coffee. Yep, he looked just as delicious in the morning. Now she'd never get him off her mind.

She moved to a bar stool and draped his robe across it. "I didn't expect you to be up so early."

"I'm a morning person."

His intense stare followed her. What was up with him? She nervously fidgeted with the Lucky Ducky keychain she kept around as a good luck charm.

When she couldn't stand to be the focal point of Lucas's attention any longer, she faced him. "Why do you keep staring?"

"It's just you don't look like the same woman I met last night."

"Is that your attempt at a compliment?"

"Actually it is. You see, my brain doesn't work very well this early in the morning until I finish my first cup of coffee." He held up a large blue mug. "But if you'd like me to spell it out, you look radiant."

Had she heard him correctly? Had a man, a drop-dead gorgeous hunk, just said she was radiant? *Radiant.* The word sounded as sweet as honey and she was eating it all up. Heat swirled in her chest and rushed up to her cheeks, but for that one blissful moment she didn't care.

"Umm, thanks." Her hand tightened around the keychain. "I'm all packed up."

"What's that in your hand?"

She glanced down, realizing she was squeezing the rubber duck to the point of smashing it. "It's just a keychain. No big deal."

He nodded in understanding.

"Do you have any more coffee?"

"I'll get you a cup."

He moved at the same time she did and they nearly collided. Kate froze, but not before she caught a whiff of his intoxicating male scent. He had on a light blue button-up with the sleeves rolled up and the collar unbuttoned. His hair was combed but still slightly damp. And his face was clean-shaven. He looked like a man ready to conquer the world.

Her heart tripped in her chest as she pictured them chatting over a morning cup of coffee and bagel. He'd tell her what he had on tap for the day and she'd tell him about her plans.

Lucas cleared his throat and pointed. "The cups are in the cabinet behind you."

She had to get a grip and quit acting like a high school student with a crush on the star quarterback. The best way to do that was to make a fast exit before she made a complete fool of herself. "On second thought, I don't have time for coffee."

"It's awfully early to be in such a rush. Is something the matter?"

"Nothing's wrong." She crossed her fingers behind her back like she used to do when she was a kid and her father asked her if she'd cleaned her room before allowing her go outside to play with her friends.

Lucas nodded, but his eyes said that he didn't believe her. She never had been good at telling fibs. That's why her father had caught her every time.

A sense of loss settled over her. What had made her think about that man after all this time? She grew angry at herself. As far as she was concerned her father was dead to her. She certainly didn't miss him.

Maybe being alone in a new city had gotten to her more than she thought. It didn't help that she'd witnessed the supportive clusters of families at the hospital while having no one by her side. That must be it.

Stifling the rush of unwanted emotions, she

made a point of checking her wristwatch. "If I don't leave now, I'll be late."

"But you haven't even eaten. Don't let me scare you off."

"You haven't. I just have things I must do." She walked over to the doorway and paused. "By the way, did you ever speak to your aunt?"

"No. I think it was too late last night and she had her phone switched off. I'm sure she'll call soon."

"I understand." But Kate still wanted that little bit of vindication. The chance to flash him an I-told-you-so look. "Thank you for letting me spend the night. By the way, there's some food in the fridge. Help yourself to it."

And with that she started down the hallway headed for the front door. She had no idea where she'd find a cheap place to stay tonight. All but one of her credit cards was maxed out since she'd been forced to give up her job to travel with Molly to the long list of specialists. She dismissed the troubling thought. There were other matters that required her attention first.

"Hey, wait!"

Kate sighed and turned. She didn't know what else they had to say to each other. And she didn't have time to waste. "Surely you aren't going to insist on searching my luggage, are you?"

"Are you always so feisty in the morning? Or

are you just grumpy because you skipped your caffeine fix? I know that first cup does wonders for me. See, I'm smiling." His lips bowed into a ridiculous grin.

She rolled her eyes and shook her head. She honestly didn't know what to make of the man. His personal hygiene was impressive, but other than the kitchen his house was a disgrace. And last night he was crankier than an old bear, yet this morning he was smiling. He was one walking contradiction.

Lucas held out his hand. "Let me have your keys and I'll pull your car up to the door so you don't get soaked."

"I don't have one." She'd left her car in Pennsylvania, figuring city driving was not something she wanted to attempt.

"Did you call a taxi?"

"I don't need one." She pulled a red umbrella from her tote. "I'm armed and ready."

"Have you looked outside? It's still pouring. That umbrella isn't going to help much."

"Thanks for caring. But I've been taking care of myself for a long time now. I'll be fine."

When she started to move toward the front door, he reached out and grabbed her upper arm. His touch was firm but gentle. Goose bumps raced down to her wrists, lifting the fine hair on her arms. She glanced down at where his fingers were wrapped around her and immediately his hand pulled away.

"Sorry. I just wanted a chance to offer you a lift. I'll go grab my wallet and keys." He dashed down the hallway without waiting for her to say a word.

This was ridiculous. She couldn't let herself start going soft. There was only her and Molly and right now, her daughter needed her to be strong for both of them. She would walk to the hospital as planned. It wasn't that many blocks and she'd already done it a number of times.

She quietly let herself out the front door, feeling bad about skipping out on Lucas. For some reason, he was really trying to be a good sport about finding a stranger living in his house. She wondered if she would have been so understanding if the roles had been reversed.

"Kate, I've got them." Lucas called out from the kitchen. "We can go now."

Lucas had never met a woman quite like her. Her tenacity combined with a hint of vulnerability got to him on some level. He sensed she wasn't the type to ask for help and would only take it if it was pressed upon her. Maybe that was why he was going out of his way to be kind to her—because she appeared to be in need of a friend and would never ask for one.

He strode to the foyer with his jacket on and keys in hand. But Kate was gone. He called out to her, but there was no sound. Surely she hadn't skipped out on him.

He stepped outside to look for her. The rain was picking up and so was the wind. But there was no sign of Kate in either direction. This was not a day where an umbrella would do a person much good.

Without taking time to question his next move, he was in his car and driving around the block. She couldn't have gotten far. And then he spotted a perky red umbrella. In the windy weather, Kate struggled to keep a grip on the umbrella with one hand while clutching her suitcase with the other.

He slowed next to her and lowered the window. "Get in."

She ignored him and kept walking. A gust of wind blew hard and practically pulled the umbrella free from her hold. In the end, she'd held on to it, but the wire skeleton now bowed in the wrong direction, rendering the contraption totally useless.

"Get in the car before you're soaked to the skin."

She stood there for a second as though ready to burst into tears. Then pressing her lips into a firm line, she straightened her shoulders and stepped up to the car. He jumped out to take her things from her.

Once they were stowed away, he climbed back in the driver's seat. "Where are we off to?"

"East Riverview Hospital."

Her face was devoid of any expression, leaving him to wonder about the reason for her visit. She'd mentioned meeting his aunt there, but she hadn't added any details. Was she visiting a sick relative? Or was there something wrong with her? Was that the reason for her drawn cheeks and dark circles under her eyes?

He wanted to know what was going on, but he kept quiet and eased back into traffic. If she wanted him to know, she'd tell him. Otherwise it was none of his business. He assured himself it was best to keep a cordial distance.

Kate settled back against the leather seat. She hated to admit it, but she was thankful for the ride. She hadn't any idea that there would be so much ponding on the sidewalks. Her feet were wet and cold.

As though reading her thoughts, Lucas adjusted the temperature controls and soon warm air was swirling around her. It'd been a long time since someone had worried about her. For just a second, she mused about what it'd be like to date the Bachelor of the Year—he certainly was easy on the eyes and very kind. More than likely, he had his pick of women. The thought left her feeling a bit unsettled.

She couldn't let herself get swept away by Lucas's charms. She had a notorious record with unreliable men. Why would Lucas be any different? After all, she knew next to nothing about him—other than he was a lousy housekeeper. He'd dismissed his desperately needed maid service. And he went out of his way for strangers he found squatting in his house. Wait. She was supposed to be listing his negative qualities.

She needed to make an important point not only to him but also to herself. "You know, I would have been fine on my own. You didn't have to ride to my rescue."

"I had to go out anyway."

"And you just happened to be going in the same direction."

"Something like that."

The car rolled to a stop at an intersection. Lucas glanced at her. His probing eyes were full of questions. Like what was a small-town girl doing in the Big Apple? And how had she befriended his aunt? And the number one question that was dancing around in his mind: Why was she going to the hospital?

He didn't push or prod. Instead he exuded a quiet strength. And that only made it all the more tempting to open up to him—to dump the details of the most tragic event in her life into his lap. No, she couldn't do that. No matter how nice he was to her, letting him in was just asking for trouble.

Afraid he'd voice his inevitable questions, she decided to ask him a few of her own. "What's the story with the house? Why does it look frozen in time?"

Lucas's facial features visibly hardened. "I haven't had time to deal with it."

"Have you owned the place long?"

"My family has lived there for generations."

Wow. She couldn't even imagine what it would be like to have family roots that went that deep. Her relatives were the here-today-gone-tomorrow type. And they never bothered to leave a forwarding address. Once in a while a postcard would show up from her mother. Her father... Well, he'd been out of the picture since she was young.

She tried not to think about her lack of family or her not-so-happy childhood. It didn't do any good to dwell on things that couldn't be changed. The only thing that mattered now was the future. But there was one thing she could do to help Lucas hold on to a piece of his past.

"You know the house is in desperate need of repairs, especially the upstairs," she said, longing to one day have an opportunity to work on an impressive job such as his historic mansion. "I'm an interior designer and I have some contacts that could help—"

"I'm not interested."

The thought of that stunning architecture disintegrating for no apparent reason spurred her on. "But houses need to be cared for or they start to look and act their age. And it'd be such a travesty to let the place fall down—"

"It's fine as is. End of discussion."

She wanted to warn him about the leaking roof, but he'd cut her off. She doubted anything she said now would even register in his mind.

With a huff, she turned away. Frustration warmed her veins. Here was a problem that could so easily be resolved and yet this man was too stubborn to lift up the phone and ask for help. If only her problems could be fixed as readily.

Her thoughts filled with the possible scenarios for today's meeting with Molly's specialist. This surgeon was their last hope. Kate prayed he wouldn't dismiss the case as quickly as Lucas had dismissed the problem with his house.

She tilted her head against the cool glass. It soothed her heated skin. She stared blindly ahead, noticing how even at this early hour, the city was coming to life. An army of people with umbrellas moved up and down the walks while traffic buzzed by at a steady pace. Her world might be teetering on the edge, but for everyone else, it was business as usual.

Now was not the time for self-pity. As the towering hospital came into view, she straightened her shoulders and inhaled a deep breath, willing away all of her doubts and insecurities.

"Which entrance should I drop you at? Emergency?"

"No. I told you I'm fine. Fit as a fiddle." She forced a smile to her lips before gathering her things.

"You're sure?"

"Absolutely. The main entrance will do."

"You know hospitals aren't a great place to be alone. Is there someone I can call for you?"

He surprised her with his thoughtful offer. How could a man be so frustrating in one breath and sweet in the next?

"No, thanks. I have some people waiting for me."

He pulled the car over to the curb. "Are you sure?"

She nodded. What she failed to tell him was that the people waiting for her consisted of the medical staff. No family. Except for Molly. She was all the family Kate needed.

"Thank you for everything." She jumped out into the rain. "I just have to grab my suitcase."

Lucas swiveled around. "Leave it."

"But I—"

"Obviously you have enough to deal with already. Besides, I'm planning to work from home today. Call me when things are wrapped up here and I'll give you a lift to your hotel."

She had to think fast. Without an umbrella, the rain was soaking her. She really should end this here and now, but she'd feel more confident for the meeting if she wasn't lugging around an old suitcase. Lucas was only offering to keep her possessions for a few hours, not asking her to run off and have a steamy affair or anything. The errant thought warmed her cheeks.

"Thanks for the offer, but I'm not sure how long I'm going to be."

"No problem. Let me give you my number."

In seconds, she had his number saved on her cell phone and was jogging up the steps to the glass doors. Thoughts of Lucas slid to the back of her mind. She was about to have the most important meeting of her life.

She refused to leave until she heard: "Yes. We will help your daughter."

CHAPTER FOUR

"I THINK WE can help your daughter but—"

Kate's heart soared. She'd been waiting so long to hear those words. It took all her self-restraint not to jump for joy. She wasn't sure what the surgeon said after that as the excitement clouded her mind.

For months now, they'd traveled to one hospital after the other. Every time she located a place that offered a possibility of hope, they were there. Now at long last they had come to the right place. The weight of anxiety slipped from her shoulders and left her lighter than she'd been in recent memory.

When a stack of papers was shoved in front of her, she glanced down, spotting her name and a very large dollar figure. Her excitement stuttered.

"What is this?" She couldn't move her gaze from the staggering dollar figure.

"That is the amount you'll need to pay up front if we are to perform the operation."

This couldn't be right. She had health coverage and it wasn't cheap. "But my insurance—"

"Won't cover this procedure." Dr. Hawthorne steepled his fingers and leaned back in his chair. "It doesn't cover experimental procedures. I'm willing to donate my time, but in order for the hospital to book the O.R. and the necessary staff, you'll need to settle this bill with Accounts Receivable." He paused and eyed her up as though checking to see if she fully understood. "You also need to be aware that this is an estimate. A conservative one at that. If there are complications, the bill will escalate quickly."

Kate nodded, but inside her stomach was churning and her head was pounding. Her gaze skimmed over the long list of charges from the anesthesiologist to medications. How in the world was she going to raise this staggering amount of money?

Her daughter's smiling face came to mind. She couldn't…no, she wouldn't let her down. There had to be an answer, because this operation was going to happen no matter what she had to do to make it a reality.

"You should also know that we normally like to treat children on an outpatient basis until surgery but with this tumor's aggressive growth rate and with it already affecting her mobility, I feel it's best to keep her admitted under close observation."

Kate nodded in understanding even though her head was spinning with information. "I understand."

Dr. Hawthorne cleared his throat. "Will you be able to come up with the funding?"

Without hesitation, Kate spoke in a determined voice. "Yes, I will."

The surgeon with graying temples gave her a long, serious stare. She didn't glance away, blink or so much as breathe. She sat there ready to do battle to get her daughter the necessary surgery.

"I believe you will," Dr. Hawthorne said. "I need you to sign these forms and then my team will start working to reduce the tumor's size before surgery."

Kate's lungs burned as she blew out a pent-up breath. She accepted the papers and started to read. Her stomach quivered as she realized the overwhelming challenge set before her.

A half an hour later, with her life signed away to East Riverview Hospital, Kate took comfort in knowing she'd done the right thing. This surgeon had performed miracles before. He could do it again. Kate was spurred on by the thought of Molly healthy once again. She could do this—somehow. She just needed time to think.

The elevator pinged and the doors opened. Kate

stepped inside. A man stood in front of the control panel.

"Five, please." She moved to the other side of the elevator and stared down at the paperwork in her hand, wondering how she'd pull off this miracle.

"Kate?" a male voice spoke.

The door slid shut as Kate lifted her head. When her gaze latched on to the man, her breath caught. This couldn't be happening. Not here. Not now.

"Chad, what are you doing here?"

His dark brows scrunched together beneath the brim of a blue baseball cap. "Now, is that the way to greet your husband?"

"Ex-husband." She pressed her hands to her hips. "I tried to reach you months ago. You didn't have time for us then. Why have you suddenly shown up now?"

"My daughter's sick. My family needs me—"

"That's where you're wrong." There was no way she was letting him walk in here and act as if he was their saving grace. "We don't need you. We've been fine all of this time without you."

His gaze hardened. "I've been busy."

After he'd refused to settle down in one place and create a nurturing environment for their daughter, he'd left Kate on her own to have their baby. He'd succeeded in confirming her mistrust of men.

The elevator dinged and the door slipped open. Kate stepped out first and left Chad to follow. They stopped outside Molly's door. Kate didn't want anything to upset her little girl, not after everything she'd been through in the past several months. And certainly not now that she was scheduled for a very delicate procedure.

"How is she?"

"The tumor is causing her some mobility problems."

"Is she in pain?"

Kate shook her head. "Thankfully she feels fine...for now. If they don't do the surgery soon that will change. But..."

"But what?"

"Money has to be raised to cover the surgery. Lots of money." Kate stood between Chad and the doorway to Molly's room. "You should go before she sees you."

He crossed his arms. "I'm not going anywhere." His voice rose. "My Molly girl will be excited to see her daddy."

Before she could utter a word, Molly called out. "Daddy, is that you?"

"Yes, sweetie. I'm here." He leaned over and whispered, "I always was her favorite."

Kate bit back a few unkind words as she followed her ex into the room. She hated how he dropped into their lives whenever it suited him and disappeared just as quickly.

Maybe that was why she'd been initially drawn to him—he was so much like her family, always chasing happiness in the next town. Having a child had been too much for her father, who'd split when she was ten. But her mother had stuck it out until Kate's eighteenth birthday, before skipping town with the current flavor of the month.

But when Kate became pregnant, her priorities changed. She wanted her child to have a real home. She promised herself that her little one would have something she never had—stability.

The same town.

The same house.

The same bed.

She wondered what it'd be like to live in a home like Lucas's, rich with family history. The man didn't know how good he had it. The errant thought brought her up short. Why should she think of him now? And why did just the mere thought of him have her heart going pitty-pat? Maybe because she hadn't anticipated his kindness after finding her, a total stranger, in his house.

"Yay! Daddy's here." Molly's smile filled the room with an undeniable glow.

Chad gave their daughter a kiss and a hug. Kate

watched the happy reunion and wondered whether she should be furious at her unreliable ex or grateful he'd made Molly's face light up like Christmas morning. A child's ability to forgive was truly impressive. And right now Molly's happiness was all that mattered.

"How long are you sticking around?" Kate asked, wondering if she had time to grab some much needed coffee and gather her thoughts.

"For a while. Molly and I have some catching up to do."

"Daddy, wanna watch this with me?" Molly pointed to a cartoon on the television anchored to the wall.

All three of them in the same room for an extended period would only lead to problems. Chad had a way of finding her tender spots and poking them. And having Molly witness her parents arguing was certainly not something her little girl needed right now. Kate struggled to come to terms with the fact Chad was suddenly back in their lives.

"I'm just going to step out and get some coffee. I'll be right back." Kate couldn't help thinking that she was a third wheel here, an unfamiliar feeling. "You should know she sleeps a lot."

"No need to rush." Chad used his take-charge tone, which caused every muscle in Kate's body to tense. "How about I stay until this afternoon and then you can spend the evening with our girl. No need for both of us to be here. After all, you have money to raise."

Just the way he said the last part let her know that coming up with the money for the surgery would be solely her responsibility. Her blood pressure rose. What else was new?

She was about to inform him of his responsibilities toward their daughter when common sense dowsed her angry words. An argument between her and Chad was the last thing Molly needed. Still, with all three of them crowded in this small room all day, an argument was inevitable.

"You can leave," Chad said dismissively.

"Yeah, Mommy. Daddy and me are gonna watch TV."

Maybe it was the best way to keep Molly happy. She caught Chad's gaze. "Are you sure you want to stay that long?"

"Absolutely. Molly and I have lots of catching up to do. Is that a stack of board games over there?" He pointed to the corner of the room.

Before Kate could speak, Molly piped up. "Yeah. Wanna play?"

While Chad wasn't reliable for the long haul, when he was with Molly, he was a good father. Kate smiled at her daughter's exuberance. "What time should I be back?"

"Three. I have some things to do then."

"Okay. I'll see you both at three." And to be certain of Chad's intentions, she added, "You will still be here, won't you? Because I can come back earlier."

"I'll be here."

Kate kissed her daughter goodbye and hesitantly walked away. She assured herself Molly would be fine with Chad. In the meantime, she had planning to do. Four weeks wasn't much time to come up with enough cash to cover the bill.

The thought made her chest tighten. She didn't have access to that kind of money. As it was, her house in Pennsylvania was being sold to pay some prior medical bills. What in the world was she going to do?

"Elaina, you have to be reasonable." Lucas struggled to maintain a calm tone with his ex-wife. "All I'm asking is for you to let me see Carrie when I fly back out to San Francisco."

"And I told you it's too confusing for her. She has a dad now—one who doesn't spend his life at the office. Don't come around again. All you'll do is upset her."

"That's not true." His grip on the phone tightened. "You know you could make this easier for her by not yelling at me in front of her."

Elaina sighed. "When you show up without invitation, what do you expect? And I'm only doing what's best for my daughter—"

"Our daughter. And if I waited for an invitation, I'd be an old man. Don't you think her knowing her father is important?"

"No. Don't keep pushing this. Carrie is happy without you."

A loud click resonated through the phone. His teeth ground together at the nerve of his ex-wife hanging up the phone while he was trying to reason with her.

The kitchen chair scraped over the smooth black-and-white tiles as Lucas swore under his breath and jumped to his feet. He paced the length of the kitchen. The sad thing was Elaina meant her threat. She would make his life hell if he didn't play by her rules. She'd done it once by skipping town with their daughter and leaving no forwarding address. This time he didn't even want to think of the lies she'd tell Carrie about him.

This was the reason he'd decided to let his daughter live in peace without the constant shuffle between two warring parents. He wanted a better childhood for Carrie than he'd had.

His thoughts drifted back to his childhood. He'd hated being a pawn between his parents and being forced to play the part of an unwilling spy. Those two were so wrapped up in knowing each other's business and with outdoing the other that, in some twisted way, he figured they never really got over each other.

But if that was love, then he wanted no part of it. That's why he'd decided to marry Elaina. They had a relationship based on friendship and mutual goals, not love. A nice, simple relationship. Boy, had he made a huge miscalculation. Even without love things got complicated quickly. Now he couldn't let his daughter pay the price for his poor decisions.

Lucas stopped next to the table and stared down at the unfinished email. The cursor blinked, prompting him for the next words, but he couldn't even recall what he'd written.

Nothing was going right at the moment. First, his ex-wife declared war if he pursued his right to spend time with his little girl. Then there was the San Francisco expansion, which was hemorrhaging money. His only hope was the launch of his newest line: Fiery Hearts—brilliant rubies set in the most stunning handcrafted settings.

The launch of this line had to be bigger and better than any other he'd done. Fiery Hearts had to start a buzz that would send women flocking to Carrington's, infusing it with income to offset the cost of getting the West Coast showroom up and running. He raked his fingers through his hair, struggling for some innovative, headline-making launch for the line. But he drew a blank.

He closed the laptop and strode over to the counter. He went to refill his coffee cup only to find the pot empty. The thought of brewing more crossed his mind, but he had a better idea—getting away from the house by going to a coffee shop. Between the hum of conversation and his laptop, it'd keep him occupied. And if Kate needed her suitcase, she had his number.

Satisfied with his plan of action, he grabbed his keys and wallet when his cell phone buzzed. A quick glance at the illuminated screen revealed it was his aunt.

"Aunt Connie, I've been trying since last night to get you. Are you okay?"

"Of course. Why wouldn't I be?"

"I'm not used to you being out so late and not taking my calls."

"Sorry. I was at the hospital, sitting with a woman whose husband underwent emergency surgery."

"Did everything go well?" he asked, already having a pretty good guess at the answer. His aunt was too upbeat for things to have gone poorly.

"Yes, the man has a good prognosis. So, dear, how are things going in San Francisco?"

This was his opening to find out what exactly was going on here. "I got back late last night."

There was a quick intake of breath followed by silence. He wasn't going to help his aunt out of this mess. She owed him an explanation of why a stranger was living here in his home without his permission. He might love his aunt dearly, but this time she'd overstepped.

"Oh, dear. Umm…I meant to call you—"

"So you're admitting you invited Kate to stay here without consulting me?"

"Well, yes. But I knew you'd understand." Uncertainty threaded through her voice.

If Connie were an employee, he'd let her have an earful and then some. But this was his aunt, the only family member who'd ever worried more about his happiness than the company's bottom line…or having the Carrington name appear on the society page with some splashy headline. He couldn't stay angry with her, even if he tried.

"It might be best if you ask in the future, instead of assuming." He made sure to use his I'm-not-messing-around voice.

"I'm sorry. She doesn't have any family for support or anywhere to go. And I would have sent her to my place, but you know after the last person I took in, my roommate insisted I never bring home anyone else. How was I to know that woman liked to borrow things?"

"Without permission and without any intention of returning them."

He was so grateful that his aunt had Pauline to look after her. If it weren't for Pauline, he'd never feel comfortable enough to leave town on business. His aunt was too nice, too unassuming. As a result, people tried repeatedly to take advantage of her to get to the Carrington fortune.

"Kate isn't like the others," Connie insisted. "She has a good heart."

"Still, you shouldn't have sent her here. This house…it's off-limits."

"I thought after all of this time you'd have let go of the past."

He'd never let go. How could he? It'd mean letting go of his little girl. A spot inside his chest ached like an open, festering wound every time he thought of how much he missed seeing Carrie's sweet smile or hearing her contagious laughter. But he didn't want to discuss Carrie with his aunt…with anyone.

Hoping to redirect the conversation, he asked, "What do you know about Kate?"

"Didn't she tell you?"

A knock at the back door caught him off guard. He wasn't expecting anyone as he never had visitors. And if it was some sort of salesperson, they'd go to the front door.

"I've got to go. Someone's at the door. I'll call you back later."

"Lucas, be nice to Kate. She has more than enough on her plate. She can use all of the friends she can get."

And with that the line went dead. What in the world had that cryptic message meant? He didn't have time to contemplate it as the knock sounded again.

He let out a frustrated sigh as he set his phone on the center island. So much for getting any answers about Kate. Now all he had were more questions.

The knocking became one long string of beats.

"Okay! I'm coming."

Lucas strode over and yanked open the door. A cold breeze rushed past him. His mouth moved, but words failed him.

There standing in the rain, completely soaked, was Kate. Her teeth chattered and her eyes were red and puffy. This certainly wasn't the same determined woman he'd dropped off at the hospital. Where her hair had once been styled, the wet strands clung to her face. What in the world was going on?

Without thinking he reached out, grabbed her arms and pulled her inside. His mind continued to flood with questions, so many that he didn't know where to start. But finally he drew his thoughts into some semblance of order and decided to start at the beginning.

"Why didn't you call?" He slipped her purse off her shoulder and set it on a kitchen stool. "I'd have picked you up."

Were those tears flowing down her cheeks? Or raindrops? He couldn't be sure. Obviously he'd have to hold off getting to the bottom of this. His first priority was getting Kate warmed up.

"We need to get you in a hot shower." She started to shake her head when he added, "No arguments. You'll be lucky if you don't catch pneumonia. If you hadn't noticed, it's awfully cold to be walking around in the rain."

He helped her out of her jacket, which definitely wasn't waterproof. Next, he removed her waterlogged red heels. When he reached for her hand to lead her to his bathroom, he noticed how small and delicate she was next to him.

She looked so fragile and his instinct was to protect her—to pull her close and let her absorb his body heat. He resisted the urge. It wasn't his place to soothe away her worries. When it came to relationships, he should wear a sign that read Toxic. And that was why he intended to grow old alone.

In his bedroom, he had her wait while he grabbed a towel and heated up the shower. When he returned, she was still standing there with her arms hugging herself, staring at the floor. What in the world had happened? Did she have bad news at the hospital? Had someone died?

Not that it was any of his business. He wasn't a man to lean on. He had no words of wisdom to share to make whatever problem she had go away. If he had, he'd have used it to fix his own messed up life. He'd have gotten his family back. The house would be filled with the sounds of his daughter's laughter. Instead the silence was deafening. He shoved the troubling thoughts away.

"Let's get you in a hot shower." He showed her to his bathroom. "Will you be all right in there alone? Or should I call my aunt?"

In a faint whisper, she said, "I'm fine."

Sure she was. And he had some oceanfront property in New Mexico to sell.

"Just yell, if you need me. I won't be far away."

While she warmed up in the shower, he rushed to the front door and returned with her suitcase. His thumbs hovered over the locks. He stopped. Opening her suitcase would be prying—something he hated when people did it to him, no matter what their intentions. Instead, he retrieved his robe and laid it on the bed, just in case she was still chilled.

Trying not to think of how good she'd looked in his robe, he returned to the kitchen. He grabbed the coffeepot and filled it with water. His idea to step out for a bit was permanently on the back burner. Once he got Kate situated in a hotel, the afternoon would be shot. And so would his patience.

He flung himself down on a kitchen chair, determined to concentrate on something besides his unwanted guest. He opened up his laptop and skimmed over his unfinished email. He had absolutely no desire to work. This realization for a renowned workaholic was unsettling, to say the least. What was wrong with him? Was it the way things had ended in San Francisco with his little girl looking at him with fear in her eyes when he went to pick her up?

He inhaled an unsteady breath. He'd made his choice, not to make his daughter a pawn between him and his ex. It was the right decision...for Carrie. Now he had to get a grip. After all, Carrington Gems was all he had left.

With one ear toward the bathroom and his eyes on the monitor, he started to type. He'd gotten through a handful of emails by the time Kate emerged from the bedroom wearing his robe. Her dark brown hair was wet and brushed back from her face and her cheeks were tinged pink from the shower.

The robe gaped open, revealing a glimpse of her cleavage. His overzealous imagination filled in the obscured details. He should have looked away but he couldn't. He was drawn to her like a starving bear to a picnic basket.

He shifted uncomfortably, fighting back this wave of desire. Sex was not the answer. It only complicated things, even in the simplest of relationships.

The fact he'd never met anyone who was so fiercely independent but at the same time looked worn to the bone only made him more curious about Kate. What was her story? Where had she come from? And what was she doing at the hospital?

He swallowed hard. "Do you feel better?"

She nodded. "I'm sorry to be such a bother."

Was this where he was supposed to step up and comfort her? He hesitated. He never was one of those soft, mushy people. He was a Carrington— strong, proud and unfeeling. Or at least those were the words his ex had thrown at him numerous times and he'd never had a reason to disbelieve her assessment. Until now....

There was something about Kate that bore through his defenses and made him want to fix whatever was broken. But he didn't know anything about comforting people. With each passing moment he grew more uncomfortable, not knowing how he should act around her.

Taking the safe approach, he got up and pulled a chair out for her. "Have a seat while I get you some coffee. Do you take milk or sugar?"

"A little of both, please."

That he could do. It was this talking stuff that had him knotted up inside. He wasn't sure what to say or do. Silence was best. Silence was golden.

Once she finished her coffee, he would see

about getting her moved to a hotel. His life would then return to normal. Or whatever qualified as normal these days. And he wasn't going to ask any questions. Her life was none of his affair.

CHAPTER FIVE

KATE SANK DOWN on the black-cushioned chair, mortified that she'd shown up on this man's—this stranger's—doorstep and fallen to pieces. The staggering hospital bill already had her worried beyond belief, but combined with the unexpected appearance of her ex-husband it was just too much. It wasn't often that she let down her guard. And she really wished it hadn't been in front of Lucas.

The steaming shower had helped clear her mind. She'd given in to a moment of fear that she would fail her daughter, but the time for uncertainty had passed. She must be strong now. Besides, she refused to fall to pieces again in front of Lucas. He must already think that she was... what? Pathetic? Weak? Looking for a handout? Or all of the above? She wasn't about to confirm any of his suspicions—not if she could help it.

He pushed a cup of steaming coffee in front of

her. "Drink this. It'll warm you up while I run to the deli and get us some lunch."

"Thank you. I'm sorry for imposing again. I…I just started walking and thinking. Eventually I ended up here."

Her hands were clammy and her muscles tense as she clutched the warm ceramic cup. Her gaze strayed to Lucas as he strode over to the center island where his jacket was draped over a stool as though he might have been headed somewhere before she showed up. His strides were long and his dark jeans accentuated his toned legs and cute backside. His collared shirt was unbuttoned just enough for her to catch a glimpse of his firm chest. He'd certainly make some woman a fine catch—except for his lack of housekeeping skills.

He slipped on his jacket. "You can play solitaire on my computer."

"I hate making you go out in the rain—"

"I was going out anyway. I guess one of these days I need to do more than just drive past the grocery store." He flashed her a lighthearted smile. "Do you want anything in particular to eat?"

She shook her head. "I'm not picky."

"I won't be long." He rushed out the door.

Kate was exhausted, but there was no time for sleep. She needed to plan out how to raise the funds for the surgery. Her lengthy walk had given her time to think and she knew there was no way a bank would lend her that kind of money. And she didn't have any rich aunts or uncles lurking in the family tree. That only left a fund-raiser. A big one!

Lucas had said she could use his computer. She pulled up a search engine and began typing. Eventually she stumbled across the fact that the Carringtons used to organize fund-raisers, some even taking place in this very mansion.

Somehow Lucas must have missed the social gene. This house wasn't fit for him to live in much less provide a venue for entertaining. If only the mansion had been better maintained, it'd be ideal for a premium ticket event.

Before she could search for alternate locations that might attract wealthy donors, Lucas returned with a large bag. "Hope you're hungry."

"Looks like enough to feed a football team."

"I wasn't sure what to order. So I got a little of this and a little of that."

They quietly set the table and spread out the food. Kate's belly rumbled its anticipation. She eagerly munched down her sandwich before Lucas was even halfway done with his. He pushed another foil-wrapped sandwich in front of her.

"That must have been some walk," Lucas said as she unwrapped the food.

"I had a lot of thinking to do."

After she'd left the hospital, she'd tramped around the bustling streets of Manhattan. She'd been surrounded by people from all walks of life and yet she had never felt more alone—more scared that she'd fail as a mother. But thanks to Lucas's kindness the panic had passed and her determination had kicked in. She would see that her little girl got what she needed—one way or the other.

"And did you get everything straight in your head?"

She glanced away, unsure how to answer. She didn't want him to think any less of her for losing complete control of her life, but she hated to lie, too. She took the middle road. "I still have a lot to figure out."

"You know, I find when I have problems at the office that talking them through usually helps. We conduct brainstorming sessions where my key people sit around tossing out ideas, no matter how crazy they might sound. One thing leads to another until we have some potential solutions. Would you like to give it a try?"

She didn't know why he was being so nice to her. A warm shower. His übercomfy robe. A cup of hot coffee. More food than she could ever eat. And now a sympathetic ear. His kindness choked her up and had her blinking repeatedly.

"Hey, it can't be that bad." Lucas squeezed her forearm.

The heat of his touch seeped through the robe, igniting a pulse of awareness. The sensation zinged up her arm and short-circuited her already frazzled mind. Then just as quickly as he'd reached out to her, he pulled back. It was as though he realized he'd crossed some sort of invisible line.

She sniffled. "Actually my life is a nightmare right now."

"The visit to the hospital—was it because you're sick?"

"I wish that was the case."

His brows lifted and his eyes grew round. "You want to be sick?"

The horrified expression on his face made her laugh. She couldn't help it. Maybe this was the beginning of some sort of nervous breakdown, but the look Lucas shot her across the table tickled her funny bone. He probably thought she'd lost control of her senses. But she was perfectly sane and this was deadly serious.

Her laughter was immediately doused by the thought of her daughter. "I don't want to be sick. But if someone must be ill, it should be me. Not my four-year-old daughter."

Lucas sat back in his chair as though her words

had knocked him over. "What's the matter with her?"

"Molly needs an operation. That's why we came to New York. No one else was willing to take the risk. But before anything can be done, I have to come up with the money to pay for the surgery."

Lucas's brows scrunched together as though he were processing all of this information. "Excuse me for asking, but don't you have insurance?"

"It doesn't cover experimental procedures. And every cent I have won't make a dent in what I owe."

His blue eyes warmed with sympathy. He nodded as though he understood. That or he ran out of kind words to say. Either way, she'd already said too much.

"I'm sorry. This isn't your problem. I only stopped back to get my things."

"Where will you go?"

"I…I don't know. I hadn't gotten that far yet. But I'll figure out something. I always do."

She got to her feet a little too quickly. The room started to spin. She grabbed the back of the chair and squeezed her eyes shut, willing the sickening sensation to pass.

The sound of rapid footsteps had her opening her eyes. A worried frown greeted her. "I'm fine."

"You don't look it."

"It's nothing. I just stood up too fast." That combined with three hours of shut-eye the night before and plodding around in the rain on top of the news that she owed the hospital a small fortune had left her drained and off-balance. But she refused to play the sympathy card. She didn't want him thinking any less of her. Then again, was it possible to sink lower in his estimation? She stifled a groan.

"I think this news has taken its toll on you." Lucas stared at her, holding her gaze captive. "Do you have family around to help?"

Did Chad count? Not in her book. "No. My mother is out of town and my father… He's not in the picture. It's just me and Molly."

"I'm sorry to hear that."

An awkward silence ensued. Hoping to fill in the gap so he didn't feel that he had to say anything sympathetic, she added, "We do okay on our own. In fact, I should get back to the hospital soon."

"I'm sure your little girl misses you."

The mention of her daughter had her remembering Lucky Ducky. She pulled the keychain from the pocket of the robe and fidgeted with it.

"I see you have your duck handy. Is it special? Or do you just like to have something to fidget with?"

Kate stared at the trinket. "My daughter gave

it to me after winning it at Pizza Pete's Arcade. She said it was to keep me company. I tossed it into my purse and eventually it became sort of a good luck charm."

"He looks like a reliable, no-nonsense duck. No quacking around."

She found herself smiling at his attempt at levity. "He's definitely seen me through some tough times. Now, I should get cleaned up. Molly's dad will be leaving soon and I need to be there when he does so she isn't alone."

His gaze moved to her bare ring finger. "You're married?"

"No. Chad's my ex-husband. And…" She shook her head, fighting to hold back another yawn and…losing the battle. "Never mind. I keep rambling on when I need to get out of your way. I'm sure you have better things to do."

"What time are you expected back at the hospital?"

"Not until three. It's best if my ex and I keep our time together at a minimum. Molly has enough to deal with. She doesn't need to see her parents arguing."

"You still have a couple of hours until you have to be back. Why don't you take a nap and later I'll give you a ride to the hospital?"

His offer filled her with a warmth that she

hadn't felt in a long time. "I couldn't ask you to do that. You don't even know me."

"You aren't asking. I'm offering. And after I kept you up late last night, I owe you this."

"But it isn't necessary—

"It's still drizzling outside. You don't need to get wet again. So do we have a deal?"

"How is it a deal? What do you get out of helping me?"

"Let's just say it feels good being able to help someone."

She had a feeling there was more to his statement than he let on. Was he wishing that someone would help him? What could a wealthy, sexy bachelor need help with?

She looked into his blue-gray eyes. "Are you sure?"

"I am. Now do you promise you won't go sneaking off again?"

She was exhausted. And he seemed determined to be a Good Samaritan. What would it hurt to accept his offer?

"I promise."

A ball of sympathy and uneasiness churned in Lucas's gut. He knew all too well the hell a parent went through when they felt as if they'd lost control of their children's safety. When his ex-wife had up and left him, she'd written only a brief note saying she'd take good care of their little girl. Until his private investigator had tracked her down in California, he hadn't been able to function.

This thing with Kate hit too close to home. But how could he turn his back on her when her daughter was in such shaky circumstances?

He needed time to think. In fact, that's all he'd been doing since Kate went upstairs to lie down. But it was almost three and he hadn't seen any sign of her. The memory of her pale face and the dark smudges under her eyes had him thinking she was still asleep. Perhaps she'd forgotten to set the alarm on her phone. Or maybe she was so tired that she'd slept right through it. He couldn't blame her.

He should wake her, but the thought of going upstairs left a sour taste in his mouth. He hadn't been upstairs in a long time. There was nothing up there but gut-wrenching memories of everything he'd lost—his family…his little girl.

Still he had to do something. He'd given his word that he'd get her there on time. The thought of a little girl—the image of his own daughter crystallized in his mind—sick and alone spurred him into action.

He moved to the bottom of the steps. "Kate!" Nothing. "Kate, are you awake? It's time to head to the hospital."

He waited, hoping to hear a response or the echo of footsteps. There were no sounds. Surely she hadn't left again without saying anything. Unease churned in his gut. No. She'd promised and he sensed that she prided herself on keeping her word.

"Kate, we need to go!"

The seconds ticked by and still nothing. There was only one thing left to do. His gaze skimmed up the staircase. He'd been up and down those stairs countless times throughout his life and he'd never thought anything of it. Then came the day when he'd climbed to the second floor only to find his wife was gone along with his baby girl. The memory slugged him squarely in the chest, knocking the breath from his lungs.

That never-to-be-forgotten night he'd cleared out his personal belongings and moved to the first floor. He'd wanted to avoid the memories...the pain. Now because of Kate and her little girl, he had to climb those steps again.

Putting one foot in front of the other, he started up the stairs. He faltered as he reached the landing with the large stained-glass window, but he didn't turn back. He couldn't. This was too important.

He turned, taking the next set of steps two at a clip. His chest tightened and his hands tensed.

Don't look around. Don't remember. Just keep moving.

His strides were long and fast. He kept his face forward, resisting the instinct to survey his surroundings, to let the memories crowd into his mind—not that they were ever far away.

Lucas stopped in front of her door and blew out a pent-up breath. He rapped his knuckles on the heavy wood door. "Kate, are you awake?"

Nothing.

He knocked again. Still no response.

Was it possible she was sick? Walking around in the cold air while soaking wet certainly couldn't have done her any good. And he wasn't going downstairs until he knew she was all right.

He grasped the handle and pushed the door open. The drapes were drawn, allowing shadows to dance across the spacious room. When his eyes adjusted, he spotted Kate sprawled over the king-sized bed. Her breathing was deep. The stress lines were erased from her beautiful face. And her pink lips were slightly parted and very desirable.

He squashed his line of thought. Now wasn't the time to check her out, no matter how appealing he found her. Relationships weren't in the cards for him. In the end, people just ended up hurting each other. And he wanted no part of that.

"Kate." His voice was soft so as to not scare her. When she didn't stir, he stepped closer. "Kate, wake up."

She rolled over and stretched. The robe fell

open, revealing a lace-trimmed pink top that hugged her curves and rode up, exposing her creamy white stomach. The breath caught in his throat. She was so gorgeous. He shouldn't look— he should turn away. But what fun would that be? He was, after all, a man. A little glimpse of her fine figure wouldn't hurt anyone. Right?

Her gaze latched on to him and the moment ended. She bolted upright.

"Lucas. What are you doing here?" She glanced down, cinching the robe closed. "I mean I know it's your house and all…but what are you doing in my room…umm, your guest room." She pressed a hand to her mouth, halting the babbling.

"I tried calling up the steps and even knocked on the door, but you were out to the world."

"What do you want?"

The question was a loaded one and set off one inappropriate response after the other. The first of which was for her to move over in bed. The next thought was for her to kiss him.

He cleared his throat, hoping his voice would sound normal. "It's time to go back to the hospital." He turned for the door. "I'll meet you downstairs."

Drip… Drip… He paused and listened. *Drip…*

Lucas turned on his heels. "Is the faucet in the bathroom leaking?"

"Umm…no."

"But that sound. Something's dripping." He squinted into the shadows. Frustrated, he moved to the light switch. "Can't you hear it?"

"Of course I hear it. I'm not deaf."

He flipped on the overhead light and spotted a wastebasket in the corner. A quick inspection of the ceiling showed water gathering around the bloated section of plaster. Droplets formed and dropped. Bits of fallen plaster littered the floor.

"What the—" He remembered his manners just before cursing. His mother had been the epitome of proper form. Carringtons should never lower themselves with vulgar language, she'd say. Especially not in front of guests.

"It's been like that since the rain started. You need a new roof."

His jaw tightened. "Thanks for pointing out the obvious."

"I told you when we met that I'm an interior designer. I know more about houses than just how to properly hang a painting."

"So you do roofing, too?"

She smiled. "No, I'm not a roofer, but that doesn't mean I can't find someone qualified to do a rush job. Because if you'd look around, you'd realize that isn't your only leak."

This time he didn't care about his manners. "Damn."

He'd turned a blind eye to the house to the point

where he had no idea this place was in such bad condition. This went far beyond the mopping and cleaning he'd envisioned. There was considerable damage to the ceiling that was now bowing, and the crown molding was warped and crumbling.

Kate listed everything she'd noticed that needed repair. Unable to bear the guilt over the devastation he'd let happen to his childhood home...to his daughter's legacy, he turned his gaze away from the ruined plaster. Kate continued talking as though she was in her element. Who knew that fixing up old houses could excite someone so much?

She got to her feet and straightened the bed. "If you want I can make a few phone calls to get people in here to start fixing things up. Maybe they can change things up a little and give this place a makeover—"

"No. I don't want people in here, making changes." He ground out the words.

A frown creased her forehead. "Of course there will have to be changes. Nothing ever stays the same. Life is one long string of changes."

The only changes he'd experienced lately were bad ones that left him struggling to keep putting one foot in front of the other. Like his last visit with his daughter in California—when she'd turned away from him because he was now a stranger to her.

"Listen to me," Kate said, moving to stand right in front of him. "You're going to have to make some decisions about this place. You can already see the neglect is taking its toll. Once it's fixed up, you can move out of that tiny room in the downstairs—"

"I'm happy there."

She frowned at him as though she didn't believe a word he said. "Perhaps then you might consider moving to someplace smaller and selling this house to some lucky family who will appreciate its charms."

He glanced around at the room. This had been his aunt's room, back when he was a kid. In this room, he'd always felt safe and accepted just as he was. This house was a scrapbook of memories, some good, some not so good. He couldn't turn his back on it all.

Ghosts of the past filled his mind. The walls started to close in on him. Each breath grew more difficult. He needed space—air. He headed for the door, ignoring Kate's plea for him to wait. With his gaze straight ahead, he marched down the hall, his breathing becoming more labored. It felt as though the oxygen had been sucked out of the house.

No matter how much he hated to admit it, Kate had a point. This mansion was in worse shape than he'd ever imagined. His shoulders drooped beneath the weight of guilt. His parents and grandparents would be horrified if they were still around to see the neglect he'd let take place. They'd entrusted him with the care of the Carrington mansion and he'd failed. His chest burned as he rushed down the stairs.

Even if he someday won over his little girl—if she no longer looked at him like a scary stranger—he couldn't bring her here. He couldn't show her the numerous portraits of her ancestors that his ex-wife had stashed in the attic. The dust. The peeling and cracking plaster. And most likely mold. It just wasn't fit for a child—or for that matter, an adult.

In the foyer, he yanked open the front door. The cool breeze rushed up and swirled around him. He stood in the doorway as the rain pitter-pattered on the pavement. He breathed in the fresh air—the coolness eased his lungs.

As his heart rate slowed, his jumbled thoughts settled. Kate was right. The house did need more repairs than he'd ever thought possible. And he was way past putting it off until another day. Then a crazy idea struck him. But could it work?

CHAPTER SIX

UPON HEARING KATE'S approaching footsteps, Lucas turned. "You're right."

"I am?" Her pencil-thin brows rose. "Is this your way of apologizing? And perhaps asking me to make those calls for you?"

"Yes, that was an apology." Why did she make him spell everything out? He thought he'd made it clear from the start.

As for having her involved with the repairs, he wasn't sure. Guilt niggled at him. Here she was with so much on her plate and she was worried about him...er, rather his house. This was all so backward. He should be offering Kate a helping hand.

Wouldn't things have gone more smoothly for him when his daughter went missing if he'd let someone in? Instead he'd closed himself off from the world. Lost in his own pain, Carrington Gems had teetered on the brink of disaster. Even today, he was still paying for the poor choices he'd made back then.

Was that the way Kate was feeling now? He glanced into her eyes, seeing pain and something else…could it be determination? Of course it was. She might have had a case of nerves earlier, but he could see by the slight tilt of her chin and her squared shoulders that the moment had passed.

Still, he wasn't quite ready to throw in with a woman he barely knew…even if his aunt trusted Kate enough to open up his home to her. Still she seemed so excited when she talked about the house. He couldn't make any decisions now. It'd take him some more thought.

He glanced at his watch. "We should go. You don't want to be late."

"But what about the roof?"

"It'll keep for a few more hours. We can talk it over when you're done at the hospital."

He ushered her out the door into the gray, drizzling day. Deep inside he knew that Kate's appearance in his life was about to alter things…for both of them. He didn't know how, but he sensed change in the wind. And after years of trying to keep the status quo, this knowledge left him feeling extremely off-balance.

But no one could understand how hard it would be for him to help this woman with a sick child— a child the same age as his own daughter…who no longer even recognized him. Regret pummeled him. He should have been home more and tried harder to work things out with Elaina, if only for the sake of his little girl. Then it would be him she was calling Daddy—not someone else.

Silence filled the car, giving Lucas too much time to think about what he'd lost and how inadequate he felt as a human. He glanced over at Kate. "What has you so quiet?"

"I was thinking about how to raise money for the surgery."

The streetlight turned green and Lucas eased down on the accelerator. "Do you have any family you can reach out to?"

"No. My family is small and not close-knit. My mother was around when Molly first got sick, but she doesn't have a lot of patience. The longer the tests and hospital visits went on… Well, now she's off in Los Angeles, or was it Las Vegas, with the new flavor of the month. She calls when she gets a chance."

That was tough. Even though his mother had remarried after his father's death and moved to Europe, he knew if he ever picked up the phone and asked for help that she'd come. She was never a warm and affectionate mother, but she did protect what was hers.

"So without a rich uncle in the family and knowing I won't qualify for a loan, I'll have to organize a fund-raiser. Something that can be arranged quickly and without too much overhead."

He paused, searching for a solution. "I'll help you as much as I can. You just hit me at a bad time as I'm fully invested in expanding Carrington Gems to the West Coast." He didn't bother to add that they'd hit one expensive stumbling block after the other with this project. In comparison to what Kate was facing, his problems paled considerably. "If I think of something that might work, I'll let you know."

"Thanks. And my offer is still open to make those phone calls. I have some contacts in New York who can hook me up with a reliable crew."

The depth of her kindness struck a chord with him. "You'd really do that with everything you have going on?"

"Of course I would. You let me stay at your house for almost a week, rent-free…even if you didn't know it. I owe you so much."

He grew uncomfortable when people started thanking him. He wasn't someone special—definitely not a selfless person like Kate appeared to be. He was a workaholic, who'd lost focus on his priorities and wound up with a house of memories and a business in jeopardy because he'd pushed too hard, too fast to gain the expansion into San Francisco.

"You don't owe me a thing. All I did was let you stay in a leaky bedroom. Not very gallant of me."

She sniffled. "You could have had me thrown in jail. Most other people who find a stranger in their house would call the police first and ask questions later."

Lucas slowed the car as they neared the hospital. Once he maneuvered into a spot in front of the main sliding glass doors, he shifted into Park and turned to her. "Listen, you shouldn't put me up on a pedestal. You barely know a thing about me. Trust me, I have an ex-wife who would vouch for the fact that I'm no saint."

"You're far too modest—"

"Don't let a little kindness fool you. I'm a Carrington. We don't have hearts—instead, there's a rough diamond in its place." His fist beat lightly on his chest. "Harder and colder than any rock you'll ever find."

"I don't believe you."

"It's true. My grandfather told me. I was too young to truly understand what he meant, but now I do—"

"You definitely have a heart or you wouldn't have been so kind to me."

"And you're too sweet for your own good."

The way she stared at him with such assuredness made him want to be that man for her. The kind that was giving and thoughtful instead of focused and driven. For a moment, he was drawn into her dream—drawn to her.

When she lowered her face, he placed a finger beneath her chin. He wasn't willing to lose the connection just yet. Her eyes glinted with... Was it longing? His body tensed at the thought. How could this slip of a woman—a near-stranger—have such an effect on him? And why did he have this overwhelming urge to pull her close and kiss her?

Without thinking of the consequences, he leaned forward. His lips sought hers out. They were soft and smooth. A whispered voice in the back of his mind said he should not be doing this. Not with Kate. Not with anyone.

But when her mouth moved beneath his, logic escaped him. It'd been so long since he felt this alive—this invigorated.

He went to pull her closer, but the seat restraint kept them separated except for his lips moving hungrily over hers. His hand reached out, cupping her face. His thumb stroked her cheek, enjoying her silky, smooth skin. All he could think was that he wanted more—more of her kiss... more of this connection.

A bright flash broke the spell. Lucas pulled back, struggling to catch his breath. His gaze moved to the window. Immediately he spotted a photographer smirking at him. Lucas surmised from past experience that the guy would take the picture and fabricate an eyebrow-raising headline to fit it.

"Wait here. I'll be back." Lucas jumped out of the car and started after the photographer. "Hey, you! Stop!"

The reporter had too much of a head start and slipped into a waiting vehicle. Lucas kicked at a pebble on the side of the road and swore.

What had he gotten himself into this time? Of all the foolish things to do. He'd been so touched by her insistence in believing in him that he'd momentarily let down his guard. He hadn't thought about where they were or what he was about to do. He'd just reached out to her, needing to feel her warmth and kindness.

How was he supposed to know there was a photographer at the hospital? And how could he anticipate that they'd be noticed? Normally it wouldn't have been a big deal, but with Kate involved it was different. She already had so much on her plate. She didn't deserve to have to put up with the press. Those news stories, as they loosely called them, were nine times out of ten malicious pieces of gossip—such as the story his ex-wife had read about him being involved with one of the Carrington models. But it had been only one crack in an already crumbling marriage.

Kate hadn't signed on for any of this media

mayhem. She didn't deserve to have her name associated with some trumped-up story. He just wished he could shield her from the public eye. With a frustrated sigh, he climbed back in the car.

"What's going on?" Kate's eyes filled with concern. "Why were you chasing that man?"

"The man was a reporter and he took a picture of us—"

"What?" Her face lost most of its color. "But why? None of this makes any sense. Why would he be interested in me? In us?"

Lucas raked his fingers through his hair. "Normally it wouldn't matter. And any other time the paparazzi wouldn't have given us a second look, but last month there was this magazine article—"

"The one announcing you as Bachelor of the Year."

"You saw it?" His muscles tensed, hating the thought of being played by her. "You knew who I was from the moment we met, didn't you?"

"That's not true." She held up both palms, feigning an innocent expression. "At first, I didn't recognize you in your boxers. I guess I was a bit distracted." Color rushed back into her cheeks. "The more important question is what will this reporter do with the photo?"

He shrugged. "My guess is he'll sell it to the highest bidder—"

"But he can't. If it gets out people will think that you and I are...uh—"

"Involved." He wasn't used to women being repulsed by the idea of being romantically linked with him. "Is the idea of people thinking we're a couple so bad?"

"Yes."

Her snap answer stung. He didn't know what to say, so he leaned back in the driver's seat. Maybe he should be relieved by her lack of interest, but he wasn't. And that knowledge only aggravated him more.

"I'm sorry." She fidgeted with her purse strap. "I didn't mean for that to sound so harsh. I'm just not used to the paparazzi. And I really don't want my picture in the news."

Now that he could understand. His family had been making headlines longer than he'd been alive and he still wasn't comfortable with it.

"Most likely something more newsworthy will come along and they'll forget about us."

"Oh, good." The stress lines eased on her pretty face.

He didn't really believe it, but there was always a sliver of hope. And right now, Kate looked as if she could use some positive thoughts.

Later that evening, Kate made sure to double-check the dead bolt on the door. She glanced out the window, relieved to find that no one had followed her.

"Anything wrong?"

She jumped at the unexpected sound of Lucas's voice. "Umm...no."

Had she imagined someone had been watching her at the hospital? Definitely not. She might be a lot of things but paranoid wasn't one of them.

"Listen, if you're stressed about what happened between us earlier, don't be." He shuffled his feet and wouldn't look her in the eyes. "It was all my fault and it won't happen again."

Kate didn't know whether to be insulted or relieved. She hadn't been able to forget that kiss either—that mind-numbing, toe-curling kiss. And he was right—there shouldn't be a repeat.

"If you don't make a big deal of it, neither will I."

He looked as if he wanted to say more, but then he turned away and headed for the kitchen. "I ordered pizza, if you're hungry."

She followed him. The aroma of tomato sauce and sausage wafted across the kitchen. "Smells good. Did you by chance order a salad to go with it?"

"Yes, I did." He looked very proud of himself as he pulled a bowl from the fridge.

"Thank you."

She sat down at the counter, still unsettled. She

kept going over the memory of that man lurking in the hallway at the hospital. She hadn't thought anything of him at first. But as the evening wore on, she'd noticed him again.

Lucas waved a hand in front of her face. "Kate?"

What had he said? She hadn't been paying attention. "Umm…sure. Whatever."

He placed a slice of the thin-crust pizza on a plate and pushed it in front of her. She didn't make a move as she kept replaying the events from the day.

"I wasn't going to ask," Lucas said, "but you obviously aren't going to eat until you resolve whatever has you so distracted."

"There was a man lurking in the pediatrics unit this evening. At first, I thought he was there to visit someone, but he stayed in the shadows and sort of watched everyone. I wasn't sure about leaving, but when I mentioned him to a nurse, he just sort of vanished."

"I hired him," Lucas said in a low, even tone.

That news had her sitting up straighter. "You hired someone to spy on me?"

"He was there to protect you."

"Protect me?" Her voice rose. "From what?"

"Remember the photographer outside the hospital?" Her hands pressed the countertop as she nodded and he continued. "I didn't want him or any other reporters to bother you with questions, so I sent an off-duty security guard from Carrington to make sure that didn't happen."

"I thought you said the press wouldn't make a big deal of it."

"I just wanted to be sure they left you alone."

"So you do think they'll go ahead with the photo?"

He wanted to assure her that she had nothing to worry about, but he couldn't lie to her. "Probably."

Her eyes lit up. "You can stop them."

"Me? How am I supposed to do that?"

"Pay the guy off. Bid on the photo. I don't know. There has to be a way."

"Even if I wanted to stop him, I don't have the man's name."

"How am I supposed to throw myself on people's mercy and ask for money after my name and face have been tangled up in some tabloid scandal?"

"So you've come up with a plan to raise the money?"

She sat back with a huff. "We're thinking of making it a costume party. Something unique. Your aunt offered to help."

"You've been talking to my aunt?"

"Since I don't know anyone else in this city except you, I approached her to help me organize the fund-raiser. Your aunt seems to know everyone, and if she doesn't know them personally, she knows someone who does. Your aunt loves to talk. We even talked about this house."

His eyes widened. "What exactly did you tell my aunt about the house?"

"Not much. Just that I found this place fascinating. The house is rich in architecture and history. I find it almost as intriguing as its owner."

"You do?" He searched her eyes as she smiled at him. Was she flirting with him? He gave himself a mental jerk. He didn't need to hook up with her. He just needed her professional expertise. "I have a proposition for you."

CHAPTER SEVEN

LUCAS HAD BEEN considering his plan all day. Kate obviously needed some immediate monetary assistance plus a roof over her head. And he needed someone to oversee the mansion's repairs—someone who appreciated its old-world charms. Kate fit that bill perfectly—if only he could forget how tempting her lush lips were.

She eyed him up tentatively. "What sort of proposition do you have in mind?"

"Since you like this place so much, what would you say if I offered you a job working here?"

Confusion reflected in her brown eyes. "You want me to work for you? Even after the run-in with the photographer?"

"Don't worry. I'll bet the article will be a small, obscure piece. Hardly anyone will notice it." He crossed his arms and rocked back on his heels. "As for the arrangement I'm proposing, it can benefit both of us."

She paused, glancing around the house. He

could practically see the wheels in her mind spinning. He'd hired enough people to know when they were eager for a position.

"I...I can't. My daughter is in the hospital and I need to get this fund-raiser off the ground."

She did have a very valid point. But there had to be a compromise. He could see how tempted she was to work on the house, and he knew from his experience with stressful situations that a diversion would do her some good.

He cleared his throat. "The thing is, I have a couple of projects with Carrington Gems that are going to take all of my time." He stopped, realizing his responsibilities paled in comparison to hers. "The real truth is I can run a business, but I don't know how to turn this mess into a home again."

A smile touched her lips and her shoulders straightened. "What makes you think I can turn this place around?"

He didn't want her taking this the wrong way, especially after she thought he'd hired someone to spy on her. He'd have to phrase this carefully. "You got me to really think about this mansion and what my neglect is doing to it. And you mentioned that you have interior design experience. So I checked out some of your prior work. It's good."

Surprise lit up her eyes. "Thank you."

"And I really like your website."

She smiled broadly. "I built it myself."

"You're a woman of many talents. Maybe I should have you consult on Carrington's upcoming web campaign."

Interest sparked in her eyes. "Are you launching a new line of jewelry?"

He nodded, not surprised that she was familiar with his company. His father's lifelong dream had been to make Carrington Gems into a household name. In fact, they still used his father's slogan—*Carrington Gems for the queen of your heart.*

"I'd love to see the new jewelry." Kate's face lit up with excitement. "Your magazine ads already have a distinctive look. I like that they are never overdone and always tasteful."

He stood a little taller. Though he had a team that put together the ad campaigns, he was an active member, adding his input here and there. He was after all a Carrington and he had a vested interest in any images that represented his company.

"I'm also in the middle of an expansion project, which needs more attention than I'd anticipated. So you can understand that I won't be available to oversee things here. However, I'm more than willing to compensate you for your time."

"My daughter has to be my priority—"

"Of course. We can work around that. Your ex-husband, is he still planning to be at the hospital part of the day?"

Kate nodded. "Actually, I do have a few ideas for the house."

"What would they be?"

Kate began listing off everything she'd like to do to the house, most of which hadn't crossed his mind when he'd offered her the job. Yet she had so much passion in her voice that he didn't want to stop her. The things he'd read about her and her work online didn't live up to the impressive woman standing before him.

As she continued explaining her vision, he couldn't believe someone could be so passionate about working on a house. His ex-wife, Elaina, had only ever been this excited about new clothes or jewels. Kate was definitely a different breed.

She paused and looked at him expectantly. "What do you think?"

"If I do what you suggest, will you take the job?"

"A good contractor can take care of everything."

Lucas shook his head. "I'm not going to let a bunch of people I've never met come in here and take over. You've already displayed your ability to take charge by getting me to see the condition of the house. You'll keep those workers in line and make sure that no changes are done without my authorization."

"I appreciate your faith in my abilities, but I can't be here every minute of the day while my daughter's in the hospital."

He knew he was asking a lot, but he needed to know that his most treasured memories were handled with the utmost care and respect. "You said so yourself—you can't be there when your ex is with your daughter during the day. I'm offering you a chance to do what you obviously love while earning some money—"

"But what if my ex suddenly decides to skip town, as he's been known to do in the past?"

"We'll deal with that if or when we have to. But this will give you something to do besides sitting around, worrying. There's nothing worse than a day filled with worrisome thoughts and nothing but time on your hands."

"Sounds like you're speaking from experience." When he shrugged but failed to add any details, Kate continued. "And what do I do about the fund-raiser?"

He'd thought about this, too. "I think between my administrative assistant, who is practically a party-planning pro by now, and my aunt, who knows everyone who is anyone, you'll have time to spare. But if you decide to pass on the job, I totally understand. I'm sure I'll find someone to oversee things…eventually."

"This isn't a wait-and-see problem. One more big rain and you'll have untold damage. You need a new roof, and who knows what else, today."

"Does that mean you accept the position?"

Kate was impressed by the speed and ease with which Lucas solved problems. A snap of his fingers and all was right in the world—except for this time.

As tempting as it was to take on this exclusive job and add it as a crowning jewel in her portfolio, she still had a much bigger problem. She needed money for the operation. And though she didn't doubt that Lucas's assistant and aunt could throw together a lavish party, it was still her responsibility. And its success was paramount.

"As much as I'd like to, I can't accept your offer. I have to concentrate on the fund-raiser."

Frown lines creased his forehead. "How is that going?"

She shrugged. "The location is going to be a problem as there are a lot of spring weddings taking up the prime locations, not that I have enough for a deposit on the plush venues anyway. I have some phone messages in to other places—I'm just waiting for them to get back to me."

"I'm sure it'll all work out."

She couldn't help but wonder if he really thought that or if he was just telling her what she wanted to hear. "Connie helped me come up with a theme. It's going to be a vintage costume party. Hopefully people will have a lot of fun dressing up."

"My aunt is a great lady to have around to help plan a party. She's had a lifetime of experience. Between my great-gran, my grandmother and my mother, there was always some sort of social function going on here."

"Really? I've never been to a formal party other than a friend's wedding."

"Not even a work function?"

"By the point where I was in a position to be invited to client parties, I had Molly to consider. I didn't get to spend enough time with her as it was, so I stayed home. We put on an animated movie and ate popcorn."

"You're a very dedicated mother."

Heat flared in her cheeks. "I…uh… Thank you."

"Don't worry, you didn't miss much at those parties."

Her mouth gaped. "Of course I did. It's a girl's dream to get all gussied up and go to the ball. You can say that because you've gone to countless parties. Just once I'd like to check it out for myself."

He chuckled. "Beneath the jeans and T-shirts, I guess you really are a girl."

She frowned. "You actually had doubts about me being a girl?"

"Not at all. You just struck me as being different from the other women I've known."

"I'm not sure if that's good or bad."

"It's neither." He cleared his throat, looking exceedingly uncomfortable. "What if I throw in free room and board if you work for me?"

The man certainly didn't give up easily. "From what I've seen in the kitchen, I'd probably starve to death."

"You've got me there. But I have all of the local takeouts on speed dial. And…maybe I'll entertain some of your design ideas."

She had to admit she was impressed, but she couldn't spread herself too thin. She opened her mouth to turn him down…again.

"No." He held up his hand to silence her. "Don't answer so quickly, because this will be my last offer and I can see the glint of temptation in your eyes."

On second thought, her serious consideration of his offer would give her license to browse around. She'd love to check out the closed-up rooms she hadn't dared explore before. "Do you mind if I look around? To see what I'm getting myself into?"

He waved his hand, granting her free passage. "Help yourself."

She jumped to her feet and hurried down the hallway. She noticed how he trailed her—so close that the scent of his spicy cologne wrapped around her. She paused in front of the double doors just off the foyer and glanced over her shoulder as though making sure he hadn't changed his mind about her nosing around the place.

"Go ahead." His tone was reserved and a bit hesitant.

She turned and pushed the doors open. This was her first glimpse of the living room and she was impressed by its sheer size. Her entire ranch house could fit in this one room with space to spare. And the ceilings were at least twelve feet high, giving the room a wide-open feel.

But there was something not quite right. She scanned the area again, taking in the furniture. Though of high quality, it was too contemporary for the house. And the impressionistic artwork on the walls didn't quite fit. A stately home such as this deserved to be decorated with items that exuded grace and elegance, not flash and fad.

With no throw covers, everything was coated in heavy dust that tickled her nose and made her eyes water. Beneath the filth, the house looked as though the occupants had gotten up one morning, gone about their day but never returned.

Throw pillows were haphazardly strewn about as though people had tossed them aside and forgotten to pick them up. Even a newspaper was spread across the glass coffee table, open to the sports page. Was that why Lucas lived like he did? Was he waiting for someone to return? A lost love?

Kate recalled him mentioning an ex-wife. Was that it? Was he still grieving the loss of his marriage?

A white-and-pink figurine caught her attention. Drawn to it, like a curious feline to a buzzing fly, she couldn't stop herself from picking it up. It was of a mother holding her baby girl. Her fingers stroked over the smooth surface. The mother and child were smiling at each other as if they'd just spent a marvelous day together. It touched something deep inside Kate and had her frowning at the thought of never spending another carefree day with her daughter.

"Put it down."

Kate jumped at the boom of Lucas's voice. Her fingers tightened around the porcelain figurine to keep from dropping it. With the knick-knack safely returned to the dust-covered end table, she faced Lucas. "You know you're going to have to learn to trust me or this will never work."

His expression transformed into one of contrition. "Sorry. I... Oh, never mind."

She noticed a deep sadness in his eyes and wondered what had put it there. But she knew it was none of her business. He probably didn't want to talk about his past any more than she did.

"The good news is from what I've seen of the downstairs, there's no damage. The rooms need a thorough cleaning and a fresh coat of paint. How attached are you to the furniture?" She tried to sound impartial just in case he actually liked the pieces.

"It can go as far as I'm concerned. Does this mean you've accepted the job?"

Oh, she was certainly tempted. "This place is so big. You know you could clear away the furniture and dance in here."

"It's been done before."

"Really?"

He nodded. "My great-grandmother started the tradition of throwing grand parties here at the house. She considered it her duty to entertain clients of Carrington Gems. She'd think up some of the grandest parties. It didn't matter the occasion as long as she could get together the city's movers and shakers to flaunt Carrington's latest creations."

Already Kate could imagine the big-band music, the beautiful dresses and glitzy jewelry. "Oh, how I'd have loved to attend. It must have been something."

"Great-gran was a crafty one. She knew these women were quite wealthy and hated to be out-done by anyone. So my great-grandfather ended up employing the finest craftsmen to design something unique for each of them."

"Those must have been some grand parties."

"They were. In fact, there should be pictures of them around somewhere." He paused as though trying to remember what had happened to them. "Then again, I think they might have been packed away in the attic. Elaina, my ex, didn't like to have antiques and memorabilia around. She called it clutter."

Without thinking, Kate blurted out, "Did Elaina by chance redecorate the house?"

Pain showed in his eyes. "I thought it'd make her happy. She made a mess of the house and…" He pressed his lips together as though realizing he'd said too much. In a blink, the glimpse into this man and his closely guarded feelings was once again hidden behind a wall. "About my offer—are you willing to take me up on it?"

Looking around the place, she was filled with ideas. "How would you feel about making a deal?"

"I thought that's what I'm trying to do. Name your price."

"It isn't your money that interests me." She worried her bottom lip. Should she do this? She had to be crazy, but what did she have to lose?

"What sort of deal do you have in mind?"

"When the work is all said and done, I'd like to borrow your house for an evening." The words poured out of her mouth like a breached dam, but at least they were now out there. "We could hold the fund-raiser here. In honor of your great-grandmother, we could have a 1920s flapper party—"

"What?" He reared back as though slapped.

"Think about it. You could show off your new line of jewelry."

"Impossible. I don't want people parading through my house like it's some sort of museum. You'll have to find another way to advertise your interior design work."

Her hands pressed to her hips. "That's what you think? That I'm planning to line potential clients down the block to have a look-see at your house? Well, you don't have to worry—the thought never crossed my mind."

She had more to say about him misjudging her, but she bit back her tongue. She couldn't forget how much was riding on her making a successful deal.

He eyed her up as though trying to make up his mind. "Maybe I jumped to the wrong conclusion. But the days of parties being thrown here are over. We'll find you another venue."

"Not one with so much allure or history. We

could double or triple the ticket price for people to come to the Carrington mansion." Lucas shook his head, but she couldn't stop. The ideas were coming hard and fast. Her hands waved around as she talked. "Think about it. This could provide publicity for Carrington Gems, too."

She didn't see why they couldn't both benefit from this production, but she could tell he wasn't quite sold. Now how would she nudge him into agreement? She didn't have a clue, but there had to be a way.

"Do you really think people are going to line up to come here?" He glanced around at the dirty surroundings.

"I know it needs a little TLC, but this place will draw in lots of curious folks."

"I don't think so."

Her insides quivered as she stepped up to him. "Please. I'll beg if I have to."

CHAPTER EIGHT

A BALL OF SYMPATHY churned in Lucas's gut. He knew all too well the private hell a parent went through when they felt as if they'd lost control of their child's well-being. But Kate was asking him to open up his home—a piece of himself—to public scrutiny. His life was already disrupted enough by that magazine article. He didn't need people he didn't even know coming in here and whispering behind his back.

He needed time to think. But not here. Not now. He turned on his heels.

"Wait!"

His steps faltered, but he didn't turn back. He couldn't. It would be utter torture to witness the desperation written all over her delicate features. Or the disappointment when he denied her what she so badly wanted.

"I'm not finished." Her voice cracked with emotion. "At least hear me out."

He didn't know what else she had on her mind,

but he at least owed her the decency of hearing her out. He stopped in the foyer and turned. The desperation on her face ate at his resolve.

"I'm sorry." She caught up to him. "I don't mean to pester you. I just… I need to do everything to help my daughter."

Lucas shifted his weight from one foot to the other. This wasn't his problem, no matter how bad he felt for her and the awful situation she was facing. He couldn't let himself get sucked back into the miserable murkiness of helplessness. Yet turning his back on Kate clearly wasn't an option either.

When the silence dragged on, Kate spoke up. "Do you like my idea about planning a party like your grandmother might have done? You know, displaying the new line of jewelry?"

He actually liked her suggestion a lot. "I'd need to find someone to wear the jewelry."

"I'm sure you must have some beautiful models on hand. Any woman would die to wear Carrington Gems."

"But this will have to be done right. The clothes and hair will all have to be choreographed to give the gems the best display possible."

"You make it sound very planned out."

"It will be. Trust me. Only the best for Carrington."

The smile dipped from her face and she suddenly looked quite serious. "Does this mean we have a deal?"

"Not quite." Though a voice inside him said he was crazy to open his home to the public, business sense told him this personalized campaign might make a big difference to the Fiery Hearts jewelry launch. "I want daily progress reports, including any surprises or unexpected delays. If I find at any point you aren't completely forthcoming, the deal is off."

He wasn't the first client to micromanage a project. Having Lucas looking over her shoulder wasn't her preferred way to work, but she'd make do. "Not a problem. I can write up a daily summary of our progress."

"I'd prefer to have these updates in person. Say over dinner each evening."

"You want us to dine every night?" She hadn't counted on that and after the kiss in the car, she wasn't so sure spending time together was a good idea. She wasn't ready for a relationship—she wasn't sure she ever would be again. They hurt way too much when they ended.

"Considering we'll be living here together, I don't see where that will be such a hardship."

"But I'll be at the hospital."

"No problem. I'm used to eating late. I'll have something waiting when you get home." He sent her a don't-argue-with-me look. "I'll let you think it over."

"I don't need to." His eyes lit up with surprise, but the truth was she didn't have any time to waste. This place needed lots of TLC. "It's a deal. Now would you mind if we went upstairs? I'd like to get your input on some things."

His head lowered and he spoke in a strangled voice. "I can't go back up there."

Not *I won't* or some other excuse, but rather *I can't*. What was up with that? She was tempted to ask—tempted to ease his pain. But she reminded herself that this was a business relationship. Nothing more.

"Lucas, thank you…for all of this." When his gaze rose to meet hers, she noticed a poignant sadness in his eyes. "Tell me, what do you plan to do with this house? You know, once it's fixed up?"

He ran a hand over the back of his neck. "Does it matter?"

"Actually it does. If you're planning to sell, then the interior should be more neutral to invite people to envision their family and possessions within these walls. But if you have plans of keeping it and living here then we can tailor everything to your taste."

"It doesn't matter. Use your best judgment."

Frustration bubbled up in Kate. She'd never encountered this problem before. Usually her clients had too many ideas—ideas outside of their budget and she'd have to rein them in. And though she was tempted to run with the utter freedom he suggested, something told her that Lucas wasn't as apathetic to the house's remodel as he wanted her to believe.

She lifted her chin and looked him straight on. "If you would walk through the rooms with me and give me a basic idea of what you have in mind, I could come up with some sketches for you to look over."

"I only have one requirement. There's a room upstairs at the other end of the hallway from yours. I don't want anyone in there. It's locked and it's to remain that way."

"But this place is filthy. You might not want to paint the room, but we'll need to clean it."

"No. I don't want you going in there. Period."

What in the world was his hang-up about that room? Had it been the room he shared with the ex-wife? Was he secretly pining for her? Somehow his reaction still seemed over the top.

Perhaps someone had died in the room. If so, that would explain why he was acting so strange. And it'd be a more reasonable explanation for turning this house into some sort of mausoleum. If she were ever to lose Molly... Her heart stuttered and a cold sweat broke out on the nape of her neck. No. She would not go there.

"I'm sorry. I didn't realize it was important to you."

He rubbed a hand over his jaw. "It's just that it's my...uh, never mind. I just need it left alone."

"I understand."

The man might be a little rough around the edges and have a few peculiarities, but she wanted to reach out to him and find out what he'd been on the verge of saying. Still, a nagging voice in the back of her mind warned her not to let her defenses down around him. In her experience, men were basically the same—unreliable.

She'd thought the moon rose and set around her father—how could she have been so wrong? She wanted to tell herself that it was because she was a child and didn't know any better. But that didn't explain Chad. She'd utterly and completely fallen for his charm and empty promises. She'd even agreed to his spur-of-the-moment proposal and rushed Las-Vegas-style I dos.

She'd convinced herself that he'd eventually settle down—once they found the right town. But no matter how many jobs he had in this place or that place, none of them suited him.

By the time she became pregnant, she couldn't remember the address of her latest apartment. She was certain when she told Chad about the baby that it would give him a reason to plant some roots. She'd been so wrong.

He'd been enraged and was convinced that she'd tricked him into getting her pregnant. He'd left that night, only to play a sporadic part in their daughter's life while he continued to chase his ever-changing dreams.

And now, at this vital juncture in her life, Kate didn't need any complications. Lucas was one walking string of complications. The first and most important was that he was providing her with the means with which to raise the money for her daughter's surgery. If their relationship didn't last—and relationships never did—the price was just too great.

"Did you see this?"

The following morning, Kate couldn't tear her eyes from the photo of her and Lucas in the paper. If she'd ever had any doubts about whether that kiss in the car had been a dream, she now had proof. But this picture made the kiss appear less than innocent. In fact, the clench appeared quite steamy—on both sides.

Her cheeks flamed as she recalled his lips moving over hers. The way her stomach had filled with a fluttering sensation. And the way he'd left her longing for more. But that wasn't going to happen. She wouldn't let it.

With a frown pulling at her face, she glanced at the photo again. Maybe the photo wasn't an exaggeration, but it had been a private moment—a lapse in judgment, never to be repeated.

Lucas didn't say a word as he sipped his coffee, which added to her frustration.

She smacked the paper. "This headline is outrageous. Carrington Heir Snared?" She set aside her steaming mug, feeling the heat of embarrassment rising up her neck and setting her face aflame. "I thought you said if the picture made the paper, it'd be obscure."

"Don't let it get to you. It's not worth getting worked up over."

"Nothing! How can you call my private life splashed in the news nothing?" Her eyes took in each and every innuendo. She couldn't stop reading any more than she could stop breathing. "This is going to be a disaster. How am I supposed to face everyone much less ask people for money when this article implies you and I are... you know."

"Sleeping together." He supplied the answer so smoothly, so casually as though having the whole world contemplating his sex life was the status quo.

"We have to do something." Her mind frantically sought out an answer. "We should sue them."

He shook his head. "First, it would only make this below-the-fold story bigger. And second, they don't actually lie. We are sleeping together under one roof—"

"But in separate beds."

"And we were seen leaving here early in the morning."

"But it wasn't the wee hours of the morning like they said."

"You're splitting hairs. Besides, did you happen to think about spinning this publicity around and using it to your advantage?"

"But I don't want publicity. I'm happy with my quiet life."

"Ah, but you're forgetting about the fund-raiser. You know what they say—any publicity is good publicity. Well, maybe not any publicity, but you know what I mean."

The scary part was that she did know what he was trying to say. And she didn't know whether to be angry...or excited.

Maybe she'd misunderstood. "Are you saying we should pose as a happy couple?"

"It's out there now. You might as well capitalize on the news coverage."

"And you're okay with this?"

He shrugged. "I know how to work the press when I need to. It's all an act for the sake of the fund-raiser and the launch of Fiery Hearts. Why not let it play out?"

She crossed her arms and pursed her lips. She

noticed how he never said that he was comfortable with this plan, but he seemed resigned to do his part to help their mutual cause. Instead of being angry with him for putting her in this position, she found herself liking him a little more.

"Kate, if you're ready to go, I can drop you off at the hospital on my way to the office."

She shook her head. "I'm not ready to put your plan into action."

"Even so, you can't let those reporters dictate how you live your life. And I promise to be a perfect gentleman and keep my hands to myself."

What worried her more was the thought that she wanted him touching her. She found she liked having him close. Her heart thump-thumped at the memory of him next to her. His finger beneath her chin. His deep, hungry gaze. His lips pressed to hers.

Drawing her meandering thoughts up short, she said the first thing that came to mind. "You should come to the hospital with me. Once I take care of the billing department, we could visit Molly."

He shook his head. "I don't think so."

"Molly wants to meet you. I told her you make the most beautiful jewelry. She wants to know if you make tiaras for princesses."

"I'm sorry. I can't meet your daughter today. My schedule is backed up." He started out of the room. "But I'll make it up to you."

"How?"

"You'll be the first to have a preview of the Fiery Hearts collection."

"I can't wait." She loved jewelry, even if it was only to admire it while window-shopping. "Don't forget to let me know when you have some free time. Molly would really enjoy meeting you."

"I won't forget. Let's go."

Five minutes later, Kate settled into the seat of Lucas's expensive sports car. She loved the buttery-soft leather upholstery, the purr of the powerful engine and most of all, the driver. She watched as Lucas grasped the black shifter. His long, lean fingers drew her attention. Her mouth grew increasingly dry. Why was he getting to her? Was it the tempting thought of what it'd be like to once again be held by those hands? The thought of a mere gentle caress had a sigh slipping past her lips.

"Did you hear me?" Lucas's deep voice jarred her from her ambling thoughts.

"I was thinking about the article." It was that darn paper that filled her mind with…things. Bad things.

He slowed to a stop and glanced her way. "Quit worrying. It'll all be fine."

She was drawn in by his mesmerizing stare. After all, he was very handsome and very available. Her heart beat faster as heat swirled in her chest and spread out to her limbs. Did he have the heater on in here or what? "Mind if I open the window a crack?"

"Go for it." He chanced a quick glance her way. "Are you feeling okay? You look a little flushed."

"I'm fine." She resisted the urge to fan herself. "Honest."

She eased the window down and savored the cool morning air. What in the world was up with her? Article or not, since when did she let a man get to her?

In an effort to act normal, she said, "You wouldn't believe how helpful your aunt has been. When I'm not at the hospital, she checks on Molly for me."

"I thought your ex was with her."

Kate shrugged. "He's supposed to be, but he isn't exactly reliable. And I don't want Molly to feel like everyone has forgotten her. So Connie and a couple of the nurses promised to call if Chad decides that sitting with a sick kid isn't for him."

"My aunt is very outgoing. She'd help anyone in need. No matter what."

Kate's body tensed. Surely he wasn't implying that she was taking advantage of the woman, was he?

"I didn't ask your aunt for anything—"

"I'm sure you didn't. She never had the opportunity to have a family of her own, and since I'm the only relative she has left, she likes to take in strays—"

"Strays! I'm not a stray." Kate glared at him. "I didn't need to be taken in. Molly and I have been doing fine on our own."

He shifted in the driver's seat. "I didn't mean that like it sounded."

"And how did you mean it?" She wasn't letting him off the hook that easily.

"I just worry. My aunt has a history of taking in the wrong sort of people—people that take advantage of her naïveté. If you hadn't noticed, my aunt goes through life with rose-colored glasses on. She can't or won't see the bad in people."

Actually Kate had noticed that his aunt was surprisingly trusting and friendly. Lucas didn't seem interested in offering more about his aunt, and she didn't want to probe any further.

They pulled up in front of the hospital and Kate noticed Lucas's shoulders tense as he scanned the area, most likely searching for more photographers. She followed his line of vision, but didn't see anyone paying them the least bit of attention.

"I'd better hurry. After I confirm some details about the fund-raiser with the billing department, I'm going to stick my head in and say good-morning to Molly before heading back to the house."

"Won't your ex be with Molly?"

She nodded. "But it isn't like we're mortal enemies."

"You aren't?"

"We'll never be buddies or anything, but we can tolerate each other…at least for a minute or two."

"And you're okay with him spending time with Molly after being gone so much of the time?"

With anyone else, she wouldn't get into this type of conversation, but something told her this was important to Lucas. "Letting Chad back into our lives is the last thing I want. But this isn't about me. This is about Molly. And she wants him, so who am I to stand between them? But it doesn't mean I trust him to stick around. Old dogs don't learn new tricks, no matter how much they might want to at the moment."

Lucas gazed past her, as though lost in his thoughts.

She got the distinct impression that his relationship with his ex wasn't so amicable. But if that was the case, why was he alone in a dusty house of memories, pining for her? There were a lot of missing pieces to Lucas's puzzle. And though she knew better—knew to keep her distance—she was intrigued by him. What was the real story behind New York City's most eligible bachelor?

CHAPTER NINE

LIFE HAD KATE in the fast lane with no signs of things slowing down.

A week had already passed since Lucas agreed to let her manage the repair work on the house. During that time, they'd fallen into a routine of morning coffee together followed by a late dinner when she got home from the hospital. Sometimes they ate in and sometimes he'd take her out. It was never anything fancy, a little off-the-beaten-path pizzeria or a mom-and-pop diner. She actually enjoyed the warm, inviting atmosphere more than if they'd gone to a high-class establishment where the point was more about being seen than having a relaxing dinner.

But when it came to lunch, she was on her own. Today she didn't have much of an appetite as she arrived at the hospital for an upcoming meeting with Molly's surgeon. They were awaiting test results to make sure the procedure was still an option. Kate had prayed long and hard that there wouldn't be any further complications.

"Kate, did you hear me?" Connie Carrington, Lucas's kindhearted aunt, smiled at her from the other side of the table in the Hospitality Shop. "I said Lucas is lucky you happened into his life."

"I didn't exactly stumble into his life. You had a big hand in that."

"I did, didn't I?" The woman smiled broadly. Her bouncy personality didn't quite jive with her prim and proper appearance. Her short silver hair was swept off to one side. Her smooth, porcelain complexion had just a hint of makeup and a pair of dark-rimmed glasses perched upon her petite nose.

"You sound quite pleased with yourself."

"My nephew needed his eyes opened before that house collapsed around him. Thank you for making him see sense."

"I don't think it was me as much as the dripping rainwater."

Connie reached across the table and patted her hand. "You, my dear, are good for him."

She highly doubted that. There was an undeniable vibe between them—more like a magnetic force. But he didn't seem any more eager to explore their options than she was to get in any deeper. Experience had taught her that once they crossed that line, there would be no going back.

"Regardless, I have a feeling the house is going to be a huge success. I just hope Lucas likes what I've done."

"I'm sure he will. It's about time that boy lets go of the past and starts living again."

This was a prime opportunity to ask about Lucas's history and the story behind that locked room at the end of the hall, but she couldn't bring herself to do it. She and Lucas were forging a friendship of sorts. If she was going to learn about his past, she wanted it to come from him. She didn't want to sneak around behind his back.

Connie sipped at her coffee and returned the cup to its saucer. "I meant to tell you that splashy headline in the paper was just the publicity we needed."

"It was?"

Connie nodded. "Tickets are going fast. A little more of that free exposure and we should be able to sell out."

Kate lowered her voice. "So you think I should go along with Lucas's idea to play the happy couple in hopes of gaining more publicity?"

Connie reached out and gave her arm a squeeze. "I do. I really do."

"I…I don't know."

"You've already started quite a buzz. People want to meet the mystery woman caught kissing the Bachelor of the Year. Many women have tried to capture my nephew's attention, but few have ever turned his head. And after the divorce, he's closed himself off. But you—you're making a big difference—"

"What difference would that be?" questioned a familiar male voice.

Kate turned. Her face warmed, wondering how much he'd overheard.

When neither of them replied, his searching gaze moved between the two of them. "Is it some big secret you're sharing?"

Kate's heart pounded in her chest. She was a miserable liar. Her best defense was silence.

Unable to look Lucas in the eye, she lowered her gaze. She noticed his sharp navy suit was tailored to show off his broad shoulders and tapered for his trim waist. Talk about fine packages. Even fully clothed he was definitely Mr. Oh-So-Sexy.

Realizing that she was publicly ogling him, she reined in her thoughts. What was she doing lusting over him? He was here to be a supportive friend. If it weren't for him and his aunt, she didn't know where she'd be or how she'd take care of her daughter.

Lucas and Connie made her feel as though she were no longer alone in this world.

"Heavens, no. We don't have any secrets." Connie's voice wobbled just a bit. "I was telling Kate that even though she isn't doing the guest list and ticket sales that she's making the biggest contribution by pulling together the venue."

"I agree. She's doing a fantastic job." Lucas gave her an approving nod. "The downstairs is all cleaned up and the painting has begun." He smiled, causing the ever-present sadness in his blue eyes to disappear. She wished he looked like that all the time.

"Now, if only the upstairs would go just as fast." Kate finished off the last of her coffee.

"I'm sure it'll all come together."

Lucas's belief in her abilities meant a great deal to her. And the fact he'd shown up today to show his support totally caught her off guard.

She flashed him her best smile. "I'm so glad you decided to take me up on my offer to meet Molly. It'll be a nice surprise for her. Wait until she finds out she has a special visitor. And I see the milkshake I ordered for her is waiting at the checkout."

"But I don't have time—"

"I'll hurry."

Embarrassed by the way she'd nervously chattered nonstop, Kate rushed away. Just because he'd shown up didn't mean she should read anything into his presence. Should she?

Before Lucas could explain that he was there to meet his aunt for their regular lunch, Kate was already across the room.

With a resigned sigh, he sat down across from his aunt. "What's going on here?"

"Kate and I were just discussing the fund-raiser. I'm so glad you agreed to do it at the house. I know that must have been a difficult decision for you, but I'm really proud of you for making the right one. Kate hasn't had many breaks. And at this moment in her life, she can use all of the help she can get."

His aunt might be far too trusting of people she barely knew and might always be looking for the good in everyone, but in this instance he thought she might actually be right. He'd observed Kate this past week, and though he'd given her plenty of chances to take advantage of him, whether by sloughing her work off on someone else or by sponging off him or by leaving him with the bulk of the housework, she'd been a stellar employee.

He shifted positions on the hard plastic chair to get a better view of Kate's slim figure as she stood at the checkout. She was a fine-looking woman. The man who'd walked away from her couldn't be very smart. And best of all, she was as sweet on the inside as she was on the outside.

He jerked his gaze back to his aunt. "And from what I understand, you're helping Kate organize this fund-raiser."

Connie glanced at her wristwatch. "Of course.

The girl needs someone to steer her in the right direction. Unless you're offering to take over."

Lucas held up both hands. "Count me out. I'm no party planner. Besides, I have urgent matters to deal with at Carrington. The San Francisco project has hit a snag. More like a brick wall."

His aunt's gaze narrowed in on him. "You aren't thinking of skipping town, are you?"

"Would that be so bad? Or don't you trust Kate after all?"

"I trust Kate. It's you that worries me."

"Me. Why me?"

"How long are you going to keep hiding and putting your life on hold? Why aren't you fighting for custody of your little girl—"

His voice lowered. "You know why. And I don't want to discuss it any further."

He thought if anyone would understand his need to do this, his aunt would. She'd saved him from being a pawn between his arguing parents more than once. He wouldn't do that to his daughter.

"But you are missing so much of Carrie's life—"

"Leave it." He fought back his rising temper. "I thought by agreeing to this fund-raiser, it'd make you happy."

His aunt's gaze needled him. "You only get one go-around in this life and it goes by in the blink of an eye. Please don't waste it."

His palm smacked the tabletop. "I'm not."

No matter how much he missed his little girl, he had to put Carrie's happiness above his own, something his parents had never done with him. And right now his ex-wife was hostile on the phone and argumentative in person. If only he could make her see reason.

Connie got to her feet. "Kate's finished checking out. You better hurry and catch up with her since you two have plans—"

"But we don't have plans. The only reason I'm here is because you insist we meet here for lunch once a week—even though I've offered repeatedly to take you anyplace you'd like."

"And you were late today. Now it's time I got back to work." Connie glanced in Kate's direction. "She's waiting for you. You don't want to disappoint her, do you?"

Before he could argue, his aunt walked away. His gaze immediately sought out the door, but Kate stood between him and the exit. He mentally ran through a list of excuses of why he had to leave. Each excuse sounded more pathetic than the last.

He straightened his shoulders. Time to make a confession. He approached Kate, who was holding a tall cup with a lid and a straw. She'd understand everything once he explained about the mix-up. After all, misunderstandings happened all the time.

She glanced up and a smile bloomed on her face. The color in her cheeks and the light in her eyes touched something deep inside him—a place that had felt dead up until now. He didn't want her to stop smiling, not now...not ever.

"Are you ready to go?" Kate motioned toward the door.

He should speak up...explain that he'd only come here to visit with his aunt. That he had no intention of venturing into the pediatrics unit full of tiny humans—little ones like his Carrie. His mouth opened, but when Kate grabbed his hand, giving him a gentle tug, the words balled up in his throat. He glanced over his shoulder at Connie, but she wasn't paying any attention as she took food orders from customers.

His gut churned. He was backed into a corner with no easy way out. Maybe he could just say a fast "Hi" and then be on his way. In and out. Fast as can be.

"I...I can't stay long."

Kate's eyes lit up. Her lips pursed as though a question teetered on the tip of her pink tongue. His breath hitched in his throat. *Please don't ask any probing questions. Not here. Not now.*

Kate's face smoothed. "We can take the steps if you think it'll be faster."

He exhaled a long-held breath. He understood the strain Kate was under...more so than he'd ever want to admit. He shook his head, resigned to wait for one of the four elevators. As though summoned by his thoughts, a chime sounded and the door in front of him slid open.

Like the gentleman his mother raised him to be, he waited for Kate to step inside. His gut churned with anxiety. On stiltlike legs, he followed her.

"Are you okay?" Kate asked, drawing him out of his thoughts.

They were standing alone in the elevator as it slowly climbed to the fifth floor. He kept his eyes on the row of numbers above the door, watching as they lit up one after the other.

"I'm fine."

"Really? Because ever since we got in the elevator, you look stiff and uncomfortable. And the frown on your face will scare the kids in pediatrics."

He hadn't realized his thoughts had transferred to his face. Willing himself to relax, he tried changing his stance and forced his lips into what he hoped was a smile.

Kate turned to him. "You know you don't have to do this. If you've changed your mind about meeting my daughter, just say so."

Apparently he hadn't done a good enough job of putting on a more pleasant expression because right now, Kate's eyes were filled with doubt. He didn't want to add to her list of concerns. After all, this was a quick visit. Soon it'd all be nothing more than a memory.

"How's your daughter doing?" He was truly eager to hear an update on the little girl, hoping things were improving.

"Today we get the results of her latest scan to see if the treatments are shrinking the tumor."

"Will that make the surgery easier?"

Kate straightened her shoulders. "That's what I'm told."

He wondered if Molly was the spitting image of her mother. Did her eyes light up like her mother's when she was excited? Did her cheeks fill with color when paid a compliment? And when she was concentrating while working with her hands, did the tip of her tongue press against her bottom lip?

Lucas drew his thoughts up short. He couldn't believe in the limited time he'd spent with Kate that he'd gotten to know so much about her.

The elevator dinged and the doors opened. Kate exited the elevator and turned back to him, still leaning against the handrail. "Are you coming?"

He swallowed hard and stepped out onto the pediatrics floor. There was no doubt about which unit they were in as a painted yellow giraffe with brown spots covered the wall, stretching from floor to ceiling, followed by a hippo, tiger and zebra. Large, leafy trees and tufts of grass were painted in the background. Someone had spared no expense in giving the tiny patients the feeling they were anywhere but at a hospital.

His thoughts took a sudden turn back to his own daughter. Would she like the painting? Did she like giraffes? What was painted on the walls of her bedroom?

The fact he knew none of these answers angered him. He should know. Any father worth the name Dad should know this about their child. Yet, Elaina had stolen those moments from him. And worse yet, he'd let her.

He used to think it was the sacrifice he had to make, but being around Kate and listening to her talk about her daughter, he had to wonder if there was another choice he could make.

"Molly's room is at the end of this wing." Kate pushed open one of the double doors.

He followed her past the nurses' station in the center of the floor. A collective buzz of children's voices filled his ears. He'd made sure to avoid kids since he'd come back from California—since he'd confronted his ex-wife.

His steps slowed. The distance between him and Kate widened. The giggle of a little girl filled his head. He paused and glanced as the child sat on the edge of her bed. She had curly blond locks like Carrie's and was smiling at someone. His daughter had never smiled at him like that. The knowledge stabbed him in the chest, robbing him of his breath.

"Lucas," called out Kate.

He meant to keep moving, but he was drawn by this little girl. Her sweet smile threw daggers into his heart. Instead of smiles, Carrie had looked at him with tears in her eyes as Elaina raised her voice, shook a finger in his face and insisted he leave.

Pain churned inside him as though someone had reached down his throat and ripped out his heart. A cold, aching spot remained. He closed his eyes and turned away from the little girl. He shouldn't have come here. This was a mistake. He needed to leave. Now.

Kate reached out and touched his arm. "Molly's room is just a few more doors down this hallway."

The heat of her touch seeped through his suit coat. He glanced at Kate. Her eyes pleaded with him. He wanted to do this for her more than he could say, but the trickle of the little girl's laughter was his undoing. He needed to get out of there. He needed to breathe.

"I'm sorry. I can't."

With that he turned, jerking his arm from her touch. He could feel her lethal gaze shooting daggers into his back. He deserved her anger and so much more.

He'd failed Kate and he hadn't even had the nerve to explain it to her. Although it wasn't as if she'd understand. Her daughter loved her. Looked up to her. Trusted her.

He inwardly groaned as the thought drove home the pain and guilt. If he was doing the right thing for Carrie, why did it feel so wrong?

Unwilling to wait for the elevator, he took to the stairs. He raced down them as though the hounds of hell were nipping at his heels.

Kate would think he was a total jerk. And maybe she was right. Perhaps there was something inherently wrong with him that drove away his ex-wife. And now his child.

CHAPTER TEN

KATE SWUNG THE hammer with more force than was necessary, missing the nail and putting a small half-moon indentation in the plaster. Just what she needed, something else to fix. It'd been two days since the incident at the hospital and she was still fuming. It was Lucas's fault. He'd made a point of avoiding her, rushing off to the office early and receiving an urgent phone call and hurrying out the door just as she returned home for dinner. He assured her it was important business, but she didn't know if she believed him.

Her mind warned her that Lucas was a typical man—unreliable. Why in the world had she let herself believe that he'd be any different than the other men who passed through her life? They said what they thought she wanted to hear and yet when it came to following through with their promises, they never did.

Lucas might clean up nice with his tailored suits and polished dress shoes, but beneath all of that varnish, he was just another lying man. She grabbed a nail, positioned it along the new chair rail and swung the hammer. Hard. Once again, she'd let her guard down and thought she could trust him. She swung the hammer again, hitting the nail dead center. When would she ever learn not to trust men?

She took another whack at the nail, shoving it further into the wall. Not about to ruin the chair rail with a ding from the hammerhead, she looked around for a nail set. Not finding one handy, she grabbed a scrap piece of wood from the floor, positioned it over the nail and swung again.

"What did that piece of wood do to you?"

Lucas. She'd know his deep, rich voice anywhere. Any other time it'd have washed over her like warm maple syrup—sweetening her up. But not today.

She didn't bother to stop and face him. Another couple of taps and the nail was flush with the wood. "It got damaged from the leaky roof and had to be replaced."

"That isn't what I meant. Seems like you're taking your anger out on that nail. Did something go wrong with the renovations?"

"No." The fact that he was acting all Mr. Innocent drove her nuts. "I have everything under control."

"Listen, I know I've been busy, but it couldn't

be helped. With the party coming up, we've had to kick up the media blitz for the new jewelry line."

So that was how it was going to be. Act as if nothing happened. She should have predicted this. Her ex swept any trouble under the carpet and pretended as if it never happened. Well, not today. Something had happened and she wasn't about to forget it.

She set aside the hammer and stood. "Don't do this."

"Do what? Ask about the progress on the house?"

"No. Avoid me and then act like there isn't a problem between us."

A muscle twitched in his cheek. "I wasn't avoiding you. Honest. My marketing director went on an early maternity leave and everyone is pitching in to pick up the slack with the upcoming campaign—"

"Stop. This isn't about your business. This is about you skipping out on me at the hospital without so much as an explanation."

"I…I'm sorry." He looked as though he was searching for the right words. "I wanted to meet your daughter but…"

"But what?" He seemed sincere and she really did want to understand. "Talk to me."

"I can't. Not now. Just please believe it had nothing to do with you or Molly. I'll make it up to you. I promise."

The little voice in her head said not to believe him, but her gut said something else entirely. Not sure which to trust, she decided she needed time to think without him clouding her thoughts with the pleading look in his blue-gray eyes.

"Thank you for your apology, but I don't have time to talk now. I need to finish replacing this chair rail."

"It looks like you'll have this place in tip-top shape in no time."

"I wouldn't jump to any conclusions yet. There's a lot to do and if we're going to show-case the tunnel, we'll need every single minute before the party."

"The tunnel?"

Kate made a point of inspecting her handiwork. Finding a nail that wasn't quite flush, she grabbed the hammer and the scrap piece of wood and gave it a whack. "Surely you know about the prohibition tunnel beneath the house."

"Of course I do. But my family liked to pretend it didn't exist. I'm surprised you know about its existence."

Kate cocked a smile. "You really need to read more often. You'd be surprised what you learn."

"I read the *Wall Street Journal* every day."

"Something tells me that prohibition tunnels wouldn't be of interest to that paper."

"Wait. Are you trying to tell me that you read about my house and my family in the paper?"

"Not exactly. Your aunt mentioned that the place had quite a history. And then I did some research online. You'd be amazed at what is put online these days. This house is just teeming with history."

Lucas raked his fingers through his hair, scattering it in a haphazard fashion. "Great. Isn't anything private anymore?"

"Quit grumbling and come check it out." She started for the door. When she didn't hear Lucas following, she turned back. "You have to see all of the work the men did on the tunnel—from rewiring the lighting to replacing the rotted wood. Although to be honest, it's more like a long skinny room than a tunnel."

Lucas let off an exasperated sigh, but she knew once he explored the hidden tunnel, he'd be as impressed as the rest of them. She led him to the back stairs that was constructed of stained wood. But it was the small landing that was a beautiful maze of inlaid wood.

"Someone was very clever," she said, coming to a stop by a sunset-inspired stained-glass window. "I'm guessing it was your great-grandfather's idea to create such an artistic floor pattern. If I hadn't known to look, I never would have guessed the center section opens up."

Sticking her finger in a discreet thumbhole, she lifted the wood panel. Inside was a rustic wood ladder.

"Don't worry. The ladder is safe. The men just finished the repairs today and I haven't had a chance to look around. You must be familiar with it."

"Actually, I've never been down there. My grandfather had the entrance sealed. I'm surprised the workmen were able to open it up without damaging the wood."

"Believe me, it took a while and lots of care. But I think they did an excellent job. Let me be the first to give you the grand tour." She didn't bother to wait for him to make up his mind. She started her descent.

Entering this rustic area was like stepping back in time. She let her imagination run wild, thinking of the old-timers trying to outsmart the cops. The Roaring Twenties must have been a very interesting era, especially for the Carringtons with their hidden tunnel.

Kate rubbed her bare arms. There was a distinct drop in the temperature down here. She was certain the goose bumps were from the chill in the air and had absolutely nothing to do with her view of Lucas's long legs or toned backside as he descended the ladder.

She gazed around, imagining the wooden racks

lined with bottles. "Back here there's a rack with some very old wine. Seems it was shuffled out of the way and forgotten."

"Interesting. Did you uncover anything else?"

"Afraid not."

He moved closer to get a better look. It wasn't until then that she noticed how tight the quarters were down there. Lucas's broad shoulders filled the space between the brick wall and the wooden shelves. There was no getting around him. And there was no room to back up.

Lucas's spicy cologne teased her senses. How could one man look and smell so good? And why did her body so readily respond to him? She knew better than to let her guard down around him. Perhaps inviting him down here was not the best idea.

"That's all there is. We should go."

Lucas glanced up from the bottle of wine he was examining. His gaze met hers. "If I didn't know better, I'd say you were afraid to be so close to me."

The problem was she liked it too much. If they stayed down here much longer, she was afraid she'd abandon her common sense and cave into her body's lusty desires.

"I...I have work to finish."

"I'm going to look around here a little more."

He returned the dusty bottle to the rack and

turned, signaling her to pass him. Anxious to make her escape, she moved. By the time she figured out there wasn't enough room for them to modestly pass, her body was sliding over his. Toe to toe. Thigh to thigh. Chest to chest.

The temperature suddenly rose. Her gaze caught his. Did she stop moving? Or had time slowed down?

"Kate." His voice was raw and full of unmistakable desire.

She'd lied to herself. That first kiss was unforgettable. The memories flitted through her mind every night. What would it hurt to let him kiss her again? Just to see if it was as good as she remembered.

Her heart pounded, echoing in her ears. Her breath hitched. She was playing with fire. She should move. Leave. Run. She didn't want to get burned. But she couldn't turn away from his hungry gaze.

His head dipped. Her eyes fluttered shut. Curiosity and desire collided, holding her in place. And then he was there. His touch was warm and gentle as his lips brushed over hers. No kiss had ever felt so heavenly. Her insides melted and pooled in the center. If she weren't pinned between his hard chest and the wall, she was quite certain her legs wouldn't have held her up.

But all too soon reality rumbled through her

dream. The memory of how he had walked away from her at the hospital shattered the moment. She couldn't do this. Not with him.

She couldn't trust him.

Ducking her head, she moved to the ladder. With lightning speed, she rushed up the rungs and hurried back to the library, hoping Lucas wouldn't follow. She willed her heart to slow. For her lips to quit pulsating. Most of all, she needed to think clearly. And with Lucas around, her thoughts became a jumbled heap.

What in the world had just happened?

Had he dreamed that one succulent moment? He ran his tongue over his lower lip, tasting the sweetness of Kate's cherry lip balm. A frustrated groan rumbled in his chest. He'd given his word that he wouldn't let something that foolish happen again. Yet every time Kate came close and he could smell her fruity shampoo and feel the heat of her touch, logic evaded him.

Now that his ill-laid plan had gone awry, he couldn't leave things like this. He started up the ladder, wondering what he should say to her. "I'm sorry" just didn't seem enough, but he had to try. With the wood plank back in place, he headed for the library.

He rolled his shoulders, trying to ease the tension running through them. He was making too much of this. It was barely even a kiss. No big deal.

When he strode into the library, Kate once again had a hammer in one hand and some trim in the other. He waited for her to turn. When she didn't, he cleared his throat.

"About what just happened, I just want you to know that I shouldn't have overstepped—"

"It was nothing." She kept her back to him, shielding her facial expression. "Now you see why I think the tunnel would hold a lot of appeal for people."

She waved off his kiss as if it was nothing— as if it hadn't meant a thing. The thought that this thing—this growing attraction—was all one-sided pricked him. His jaw tightened and his body tensed. Why was she being this way? He wasn't the only one who felt something.

Kate swung around to face him with the hammer still in her hand. "Do you have a problem with the plans?"

Lucas found himself eyeing the business end of the hammer. If she meant to gain his attention, she'd certainly done that. Not that he couldn't easily overpower her. After all, she was inches shorter than him and looked to be as light as a feather. Only feathers didn't have so many delicious curves. Kate's waist dipped in above the flare of her hips, and his fingers itched to wrap around her and pull her close. He was tempted to remind her that though the kiss had been brief, it'd definitely ignited a flame.

He straightened his shoulders. "And what if I do have a problem with all of this?"

"You're backing out on me now?" Kate's features hardened and he couldn't help but notice how her knuckles turned white as her grip on the hammer tightened. "You can't do that. I won't let you. We have a verbal agreement. If you even think of backing out now, I'll…I'll…"

He smothered a chuckle as her threat lost steam. Not wanting to add fuel to her rising temper, he willed his lips not to lift into an amused grin. She sure was cute when she was worked up. Maybe it wouldn't hurt to egg her on a little more.

"Should I be worried?"

"You already agreed to this party. It's too late to back out now. I already gave my word to the hospital that I'd have the funds for the operation."

Her words hit him with more sting than any blow from a hammer. She was right. How was he supposed to put up an argument now when faced with a little girl's well-being?

As though remembering the hammer was still in her hand, Kate bent over and placed it on the white drop cloth lining the floor. She straightened and tilted her chin upward. "Besides, your aunt thinks the prohibition tunnel will play in nicely with the 1920s flapper theme."

"That's what I'm afraid of," he mumbled.

As though he hadn't spoken a word, Kate continued, "She also said that at last some good would come from the Carrington history."

He didn't like being ganged up on by his aunt and his... What was Kate to him? A friend? She was closer to him than he let anyone get these days. But *friend* didn't seem to fit what they had either. Especially not after that brief but stirring kiss.

Just then Kate leaned toward him. He froze. What was she planning to do? His gaze slipped down to her lips. They were full and rosy, just perfect for another sweet kiss. Anticipation grew. Was it possible she'd enjoyed his touch more than she'd been letting on?

His breath hitched as she moved closer. Her hand reached out to him. What was she going to do? Pull him down to her?

The thought of her being so bold...of her taking control of the situation turned him on. His eyes drifted closed. All semblance of logic fled his brain. He waited for her to make her move, willing her to keep going.

Long-ignored desires roared through his heated veins. After all, they were alone and it was late in the evening. No one would bother them until morning. And it had been so long since he'd let his defenses down—since he'd been close with anyone.

"There. All taken care of."

Lucas's eyes sprang open. What was taken care of? Certainly not his needs—his desires.

"Don't worry." Kate held out a white piece of fuzz for his inspection. "At first, I was worried that it was some spackling, but it's just lint. Your suit has been saved."

His suit? That wasn't what he was concerned about at this moment. His clothes might be fine, but his mind and body were a jumbled mess. He swallowed hard, working hard to control his wayward thoughts.

"Why are you working so late?" His voice came out much harsher than he'd intended.

Kate's brown eyes flashed with surprise. "I had things to do."

"You're supposed to be overseeing the project, not doing all of the work yourself."

Her hands pressed against her slender hips and her eyes narrowed in on him. "I'm doing what needs to be done. Unlike some people in this room, I keep my word."

Her barbed comment didn't go unnoticed by him. She was still ticked at him about the episode at the hospital. He should explain to her what had happened. But that would only lead to more questions…questions he didn't want to answer.

Not now.

Not ever.

When he didn't respond, she added, "You know, if you didn't want to meet my daughter, all you had to do was say so in the first place."

"But I wanted to—"

Lucas stopped. His jaw tightened, his back teeth grinding together. What was he saying? This wasn't going to make things better for either of them. But the damage had been done.

An inquisitive gleam showed in her eyes. "What do you mean you wanted to? Why'd you change your mind?"

He glanced away and shuffled his feet. His gut told him that she wasn't going to drop the subject until he fessed up. But how could he do that? He didn't talk about his past with anyone…not even his aunt.

"Surely you have something to say for yourself." Her tone was hard and sharp.

He didn't like being pushed around. His ex-wife had known his vulnerabilities and used them for her own benefit. He wouldn't allow someone else to take advantage of him again.

Kate could push and shove as hard as she wanted, but he wouldn't give in…not until he was ready.

"I'm tired. And I still have reports to go over.

There's Chinese takeout on the counter if you want some. And just so you know, I am truly sorry."

He turned away from the confused look in her eyes, telling himself that he didn't care. This woman meant absolutely nothing to him.

Nothing. At. All.

But if that was the case, why as he yanked the door shut behind him did he feel like a total heel? And why did he want a chance to make things right with her?

CHAPTER ELEVEN

HE'D TOTALLY OVERREACTED.

So what if he'd lost his mind for a moment and kissed her again? It didn't mean he was falling for her big brown eyes or her cherry lips. The whole lack of judgment thing could be written off to a few restless nights and the stress of not bringing in enough money to cover the overages regarding the San Francisco expansion.

Days passed and with each day that went by, Lucas noticed that they were falling back into an easy routine. Pretending they hadn't shared yet another even more intense lip-lock seemed to work during the day, but at night, when he should be sleeping, images of Kate and her tempting kisses filled his thoughts.

"Sorry I'm late." She rushed into the kitchen after returning from her visit to the hospital. "You didn't have to wait to eat. In fact, I'm not really hungry."

"I have plans for us tonight. Instead of the food coming to you, you are going to the food."

She shook her head before sinking down onto a kitchen chair. "I'm sorry. I'm too tired to go anywhere."

Dark shadows under her eyes sent up warning flares. Maybe asking her to work on the house was too much for her.

He realized that in his attempt to avoid his unwanted attraction to her, he'd failed to do his duty as her boss—and, dare he admit it, as her friend. He'd let her work herself into the ground while he'd been busy at the office. He had to fix this, but how?

"No problem. When you get your appetite back, I'll get you whatever you want." He sat down next to her. "Your wish is my command."

With her elbows propped on the table, she rested her chin on her upturned palms. Was it exhaustion that had her so down? Or did she have bigger things on her mind? Was it Molly? Had her health taken a turn for the worse? His chest tightened.

"How's Molly today?"

Kate's eyes widened. "How did you know that's what I had on my mind?"

"What else would you be thinking about?" Unlike him, she probably hadn't fantasized the afternoon away, imagining the temptation of another kiss.

"Molly's refusing the surgery."

This news set him back. "What do you mean refusing?"

"Well, she didn't put it in those terms. But she's moody and depressed. She's insisting on going home and I can't blame her. She's been poked, prodded and examined for months now."

He'd have a hard time dealing with that and he was an adult. He didn't know how a child could put up with visiting doctor after doctor. Children were supposed to be outside, running around in the fresh air playing dodgeball or jumping rope, whatever it was that little girls liked to do.

"I'm sorry. That can't be easy for either of you. Did you tell her that it won't be much longer?"

Kate nodded. Her eyes glistened with unshed tears. "What am I going to do? They say with tricky surgeries that the patient's attitude plays a huge role in the recovery."

He didn't have any experience with sick people or surgeries. He'd been a kid when his grandparents passed on. And his father died of a massive coronary at his desk at the Carrington offices. So all he could do was try to remember what it felt like to be a kid. And his favorite memories were of the times when he'd been with his aunt.

A thought sprang to mind. "Why don't you give Molly something to look forward to?"

Kate narrowed her gaze on him. "Don't you think that's what I've been trying to do?"

"You aren't understanding me. What if you give her something to dream about? A plan for when she gets out of the hospital?"

"I'm running low on brilliant ideas. And by the time Molly is out of the hospital, I won't have two pennies to rub together much less money for a trip to Disneyland."

This was a small way he could help Kate. "You don't have to spend a lot to make your little girl happy. And you don't have to visit Sleeping Beauty Castle either."

Kate jerked upright. "How would a bachelor like yourself know about Sleeping Beauty Castle?"

He wasn't about to tell her that he too had a little girl and when he used to read her bedtime stories, he'd promised to take her there when she got a little older.

"Who doesn't know about the castle?" he bluffed. "It's in almost every Disney commercial. But what I was trying to say is that you don't need that. You could plan a whole vacation right here in New York City."

"You may not notice the cost, but dinners out and show tickets add up quickly."

"But there are other options."

Kate rolled her eyes. "If you are going to tell me to take Molly window-shopping, save your breath. That will never fly. She'll want everything she sees."

"I can assure you that good times don't have to cost a fortune."

"And what would you know about it? You probably grew up with the proverbial silver spoon in your mouth."

"You might be surprised to know that my childhood didn't have as many silver spoons as you'd imagine."

She paused and eyed him up. "There's no way you're going to convince me that your family sent you out into the world to earn bread money."

Her words pricked his good mood, deflating it. "Money isn't everything. Sometimes I think it would have been better to be born into a different family, one who didn't worry so much about money and appearances. Maybe then my parents wouldn't have…"

"Wouldn't have what?"

He glanced up to find genuine concern in her eyes. He hadn't meant to open this door to his past. Some things were best unsaid. But in this one particular case, his past might show Kate just how good she and her daughter have it.

He sighed. This still wasn't going to be easy. "Maybe without Carrington Gems and the status that came with it, my parents wouldn't have gotten divorced. But even after they got divorced, things didn't get much better. They still fought, mostly over me."

"I'm sorry."

Not about to get into how they'd turned him into a spy for each of them, he continued, "It was during this period that my aunt would whisk me away. She could see that I wasn't happy. So she'd take me on day trips around the city."

Kate waved away his idea. "I'm sure it was nice. But if I want to distract Molly and give her something to look forward to, it's got to be better than a walk in the park and a push on the swings. Besides, when she gets out of the hospital, we'll be heading back to Pennsylvania. This job is great, but it'll be over soon. I have to think about either getting my old position back or finding a new one."

He frowned at the thought that one day soon Kate would be gone. He was getting used to having her around. Not that he was getting attached to her or anything. He just liked having someone at home with whom to share a meal and make conversation.

Still, he'd like to see that Kate and her daughter had good memories to take home with them. His idea would take some convincing. However, seeing something with one's own eyes was always more persuasive than a sales pitch.

Yes, that's what he'd do—show Kate a good time.

* * *

The next morning, Kate was back working in the library, mulling over how to cheer up Molly. She liked that Lucas had been there pitching helpful ideas. Most of all, she liked that he'd opened up some about his childhood. Things must have been bad if his aunt felt she had to get him out of the house. Her heart went out to that little boy who'd been in such an unhappy situation.

"Let's go."

Her head jerked up at the sound of Lucas's voice. "What are you doing here?"

"I came to pick you up."

She straightened, not recalling that they'd had any plans. Yet he was standing there midmorning in a dark pair of jeans, which accented his athletic legs, and he'd unbuttoned his blue collared shirt and rolled up the sleeves. What in the world had gotten into him? And why did she find herself staring at him like some starstruck highschooler? Probably because it should be against the law to look that good.

His blue eyes twinkled with mischief. "Well, are you just going to stand there smearing paint everywhere?"

She glanced down, finding the paint stick she'd been using to stir the white paint for the trim dripping all over the drop cloth. She hurried to set it aside and put the lid back on the can. Something told her that she wouldn't be doing any painting until Lucas left, not if she wanted to get the paint on the walls and not the floor.

That was one thing about this project that she really enjoyed, being able to work with her hands. At her old job she'd done the sketches, consulted with the owners and supervised the transformation. But she hadn't rolled up her sleeves and dived in with the detail work. When she finished with this project, it truly would be the crowning accomplishment in her portfolio. First, though, she had to get it finished. Too many things were riding on her bringing this project in on schedule.

"I can't go anywhere. I have work to do." She pressed her hands to her hips.

"You need a break."

"What I need is a few more hours in the day."

"I thought you might say that so I'd like you to meet Hank and Mike." Two men in white overalls stepped into the doorway. "They can paint or whatever it is you need them to do."

"But I can't just leave."

Lucas grabbed her hand and pulled her toward the door. "We have to hurry—"

"Is it Molly? Did something happen—"

"No. Nothing like that. This is all good. I promise." He sent her a reassuring smile that made her stomach dip. "Go get changed while I make a quick phone call. We have someplace to be."

"I need to have a few words with these guys."
Lucas frowned.

"It'll only take a minute."

"Hurry." He turned and strode away.

Minutes later, dressed in fresh jeans and a pink blouse, Kate stepped outside. The bright sunshine warmed her skin. With just a gentle breeze, it was warm enough to venture out without a jacket.

As they made their way down the sidewalk, she couldn't hold back her curiosity. She stepped in front of Lucas and turned. "I'm not going any further until you tell me where we're headed."

"Didn't your mother ever teach you to wait patiently for your surprise?"

"My mother didn't do surprises. Let's just say she had an active social life and kids didn't really fit into the equation."

Lucas's lips pressed into a firm line. "If it makes you feel any better, I know where you're coming from. My mother wasn't big into the parenting scene either, unless it fit some sort of social agenda."

Their conversation dwindled as they started to walk again. Destination unknown. Kate gave up worrying about it and lifted her face up to the sun. The exercise and the sunshine were working wonders on her mood. The tension in her neck and shoulders eased away.

In no time at all, Lucas was taking her by

the hand and leading her through Central Park. "Come on."

This was his surprise? A trip to the park? Her good mood dimmed as she thought of how much Molly would enjoy this adventure. "What are we doing here?"

"I'll show you." He led her over to a beautiful white horse-drawn carriage and held out his hand. "We're going for a ride."

"Are you serious? But why?" She hesitated. "I shouldn't be here."

Lucas's dark brows drew together. "Why?"

"Because it isn't right. Not with Molly in the hospital."

He nodded as though he understood. "I guess I didn't think this through. Would you rather go see her?"

"Yes…but I can't. This is Chad's agreed time with her. And she likes having her dad around. And I…I don't do so well with his occasional snide little comments."

"Well, since you can't see Molly yet, consider this a research project."

"Research?"

"Sure. I'm showing you how to have a good time without spending a fortune. You didn't believe me so I decided to show you."

"This can't possibly be that cheap."

"You'd be surprised. It's actually reasonable.

Although the price does go up if you reserve a carriage for a specific time or have some extras thrown in."

Kate was impressed as she climbed in the carriage with a plush red interior. The driver, all decked out in white tails and a hat, closed the door for them. Instead of fighting it and thinking of everything she should be doing, she settled back on the seat and enjoyed the moment.

Now, she truly felt like Cinderella. Wait, that would make Lucas her Prince Charming, and she'd already decided that could never be. As the horses' hooves clipped along, she shoved the troubling thought to the back of her mind. Why ruin this one magical moment with reality?

A few minutes later, Lucas leaned over to whisper in her ear. "Are you enjoying your surprise?"

His breath tickled her neck, sending an army of goose bumps down her arms. "I am." The admission rolled easily off her tongue. "But I don't know if Molly would be excited about a carriage ride."

"Sure she would. What little girl wouldn't want to ride in a horse-drawn carriage?"

"Perhaps."

"I guess I'll just have to work a little harder. I'm sure I can come up with an idea or two sure to impress a little girl and a big one, too."

Kate's stomach fluttered. Maybe it wouldn't be

so bad to let herself imagine that Lucas was her Prince Charming and this was the carriage taking her to the ball. After all, fairy tales weren't true. Everyone knew that. This would just be pretend.

When Lucas stretched his arm out behind her, she gave in to the dream and leaned back. Her head rested on him and shivers of awareness cascaded down her spine. She closed her eyes, willing this moment to go on and on. They could just keep going, leaving their troubles behind. A smile tugged at the corners of her lips as she envisioned them riding off into the sunset together. If only fairy tales came true...

"And what has you smiling?"

Kate's eyelids fluttered open. She'd been busted. It was almost as if he could read her thoughts, but even if he could, there was no way she'd confirm how she'd been daydreaming about him pulling her closer and pressing his lips to hers.

She crossed her fingers before telling a fib like she'd done as a child. "Just enjoying the day."

All too soon the ride was over. Lucas gave her a hand down. It was then that she realized they hadn't stopped in the same spot where they'd started.

"It's time for lunch and I know the perfect thing to have on our outing."

He treated her to a hot dog with the works.

They settled on a park bench and quietly ate while the world went by without any notice of them. When they'd finished, Lucas took her by the hand and they started walking. He smiled, appearing very relaxed. She hadn't seen him in this good of a mood since...well, ever.

After they'd walked a little ways, she couldn't contain her curiosity. "Where are we going now?"

"You'll see in just a moment."

Soon carousel music lilted through the air, giving the day a surreal feeling as though all was right in the world.

"Come on." He pulled her closer to the colorfully painted merry-go-round.

"Why?"

"You'll see."

How could she resist when he looked like an excited child himself? Laughter bubbled up in her throat, and she let him lead her by the hand. But when he paid for her to ride the merry-go-round, she hesitated.

"I can't ride that."

"Why not?"

"It's for kids."

"Are you trying to tell me that you aren't a kid at heart? Besides, you wanted examples of things you can do with Molly on a budget. This is one of them."

"True." She really did like the idea. She'd been

to a carnival as a little kid with her father and she'd loved riding the carousel, especially the horses that went up and down. "But that doesn't mean that I have to ride one."

"Give me your phone."

"What? Why don't you use your own?"

"It will be simpler this way."

"What will?" The man certainly wasn't explaining himself very well today.

"I'm going to take some photos for you to show Molly."

"I don't know." What would Molly think? Her mother off playing without her. Guilt riddled her. "What if it upsets her?"

"You have a good point." Then he snapped his fingers. "I've got it. Just don't show her the pictures with you in them. And make sure you promise to bring her here as soon as she's healthy enough."

Kate wasn't so sure. But so far nothing else was helping to cheer up her little girl. Even the surprise of her father showing up had worn off. Kate was getting desperate to give her daughter hope. Maybe Lucas was right. Maybe this outing would give her the ability to paint a picture in her daughter's mind of the fun things they could do...together.

She wouldn't be an absentee parent like her father...or her mother. Even though they had shared the same house, her mother had been so wrapped up in her own world that she'd never had time for Kate.

She glanced over at Lucas. What would he be like as a father? Probably terrific, if today was any indication. Not that she would be sticking around to find out.

While riding the merry-go-round, she noticed a small crowd forming nearby. Cameras were flashing. It took her a couple of passes to realize they were talking to the city's mayor and his young family, who were most likely campaigning.

A niggling thought started to churn in her mind. Something Connie had said about a little more press coverage and they'd have a sold-out venue. With all of those reporters, it surely wouldn't be that hard to get coverage, but it would have to be something really good.

When she got off the ride, Lucas was waiting for her with a bouquet of balloons fastened to his hand. One of the reporters sent an inquisitive look in Lucas's direction. So his Bachelor of the Year status was still giving him quite a bit of notoriety, or was Lucas Carrington normally that notable of a figure in the Big Apple? Which left her wondering if she should play upon his fame—after all, it was for a good cause.

He smiled, looking proud of himself. "Admit it. You had fun."

"Yes, I did. You've made this an amazing day. Thank you."

He handed over the bouquet of rainbow-colored balloons. "Does this mean I'm forgiven for being a jerk the other day?"

He had really hurt her, but the more she got to know him, the more she realized he truly was a good guy.

"It depends…" When his gaze dipped to her lips, her thoughts scattered.

"Maybe this will help convince you."

Lucas's hands wrapped around her waist, pulling her closer. She willingly obliged. Her breath locked in her chest as she waited. Hoping. Longing.

It that moment, the world slipped away. It was just the two of them on this enchanted day. His head lowered. Her chin tilted upward.

CHAPTER TWELVE

LUCAS SHRUGGED OFF the glances he kept getting from some of the paparazzi. He wouldn't let them ruin this day. Normally he would have quietly slipped away with Kate. But he'd agreed to play up this relationship in public, so there was no need to deny he was enjoying Kate's company. And there was no need to resist what he'd been dying to do all afternoon...

His lips sought hers. The more he tasted her, the more he desired her. When she kissed him back, he forgot their circumstances, their differences and even where they were. The fact she desired him was a powerful aphrodisiac. Her kisses were even more arousing in person than they were in his dreams. A moan swelled in his throat.

Kate startled him when she pressed her hands to his chest and pushed. She broke free of his hold and stared up at him with rosy cheeks and a questioning stare.

"Lucas, people are staring."

So much for staying calm, cool and collected around her. He should probably apologize…again, but this time he wasn't sorry. He'd enjoyed holding her close and he didn't notice her complaining.

"That guy over there," she pointed to a young man who met Lucas's gaze straight on, "I think he took our picture."

Lucas glanced back but the man had disappeared into the crowd. "Good."

"Good?"

"Yes. Remember you and I are playing the happy couple for the press. So turn that frown upside down."

She smiled, but he could tell it was forced. Was she unhappy about the kiss? Impossible. She'd been an active participant. Maybe it was the fact they'd end up making headlines again. She hadn't been too thrilled with it the first time around. It was best not to say anything.

"How about some ice cream before we head back?" He could really deal with something icy cold about now.

A little bit later, they headed back to the house and Lucas couldn't believe what a wonderful day they'd shared. Thanks to Kate, he'd let loose and laughed. He'd truly enjoyed himself.

Kate's hand was wrapped with the ribbons of six helium balloons. A rainbow of colors. All for Molly. In Kate's other hand, she was holding a strawberry ice cream cone. He couldn't turn away as her tongue darted out and slowly made a trail up the creamy surface. There was no point in continuing to deny the chemistry running between them. And he knew by the way she'd eagerly returned his kiss that she felt it too.

He couldn't wait for later tonight. A little dinner after she got home from the hospital. Some conversation. And then, well, he'd let nature take its course.

"What are you grinning about?" Kate shot him a curious stare.

"I'm just basking in the glow of your happiness."

"Seriously? You really do know how to lay it on thick, don't you?"

"Sometimes it works."

"So what you're saying is that you make a habit of seducing women with horse-drawn carriages and rides on the carousel."

He truly enjoyed this playful side of Kate. "Afraid I've been busted. But in my defense, you did enjoy yourself."

She gave a nonchalant shrug, but he noticed the smile she was fighting to hold back. He liked making her happy. He liked it a lot.

She glanced up at him. "Truthfully I haven't had this much fun since I was a kid."

"Did your parents take you to an amusement

park?" He was genuinely interested in learning more about her.

"No. But my dad used to take me to the fire department's summer carnival."

"Sounds like a nice memory. Do you keep in touch with your father?"

She frowned and shook her head. "That's all in my past. I learned long ago to keep looking forward. Nothing good comes from glancing back."

"Memories are important." His thoughts drifted back to the time he'd spent with his little girl. "I don't know what I'd do without them. What was your childhood like?"

Kate picked up her pace. What was it about her past that could change her mood so rapidly? Didn't they say that keeping things bottled up only caused them to fester and the only way to heal was to let it all out?

"Talk to me, Kate."

"You aren't going to drop this, are you?"

"Not until you tell me a little about your past… your father."

She stopped suddenly and glared at Lucas. "My father turned his back on a ten-year-old girl who worshipped the ground he walked on, and he didn't so much as say goodbye."

"Surely he didn't just walk away without a reason?"

Kate huffed and started walking again. "Floyd

loved surprises. And his biggest surprise of all was disappearing from my life."

"But before he left, you two were close, what with the memory of the carnival and I'm guessing there must be others."

"What does it matter?" When a large black dog on a much too long leash approached them, Kate dodged in front of Lucas, giving the dog a wide berth. Once they passed the overly friendly four-legged canine, she slowed her pace. "I don't know why we're talking about him. I told you, it's ancient history."

Lucas didn't understand why all of a sudden this had become so important to him, but he couldn't let the subject drop. "Are you saying he was a bad parent?"

She stopped and pressed her hands to her hips. With her shoulders squared, she tilted her chin. "Actually it's the opposite—Floyd was a good father. We had a lot of fun together. He made up for my mother's lack of interest."

"I wish my father had been more like yours. He spent all of his time at the office and left me at home with the nanny, unless my aunt took pity on me, dressed me up and took me out."

"I guess we both came up short in the parenting department."

Lucas looked up, spotting a silver car going much too fast. Kate was too busy talking to him to notice. When she went to step off the curb, he grabbed her arm, pulling her back. She lost her balance and fell against him.

Her body seemed to fit naturally against his. He wanted to keep her safe next to him. But more than that he wondered who she leaned on—who watched out for her. He didn't like thinking of her all alone in the world.

Kate glared at him and moved away. "What did you do that for?"

"You almost stepped in front of that car."

"Oh. I didn't see it."

It was probably his fault. He was pushing her too hard to open up, but he couldn't stop the flow of questions. He needed to know a little more. "So what happened to your father? Why did he just up and leave?"

She sighed. "He and my mother fought a lot, but it was always behind closed doors so I don't know what they argued about that last night. My mother would never talk about it. When I woke up, he was gone. He never came back. And my mother refused to answer my questions. Finally, I quit asking."

As her words sunk in, Lucas's gut knotted. He realized why this conversation was important. He wondered what his little girl would one day say about him. But Carrie wouldn't even have the benefit of good memories. Then again, she wouldn't have the horrid thoughts of being a pawn between her parents—nor the overwhelming guilt from spying on one parent for the other. When his daughter was old enough to understand, she'd realize he'd made a very difficult decision in order to spare her. It was this knowledge that got him through the long, lonely evenings and the depressing holidays. He was doing what was best for Carrie.

He reached for Kate's hand and gave it a squeeze. "I'm sure there has to be a logical answer to what happened—"

"That makes one of us. There's no excuse for just abandoning your child."

The raw edge in her voice cut him deeply. His fingers released her hand. He struggled to keep walking. Was this animosity the way his daughter would feel about him?

Before he could catch his breath, Kate continued. "The only excuse is that he never loved me. He tossed me aside like yesterday's garbage. Men like him are as low as pond scum. No. Lower."

The ice cream churned in his stomach. All Lucas could muster was a nod.

Not love her? Lucas couldn't imagine anyone being able to resist Kate's smile or her teasing ways. But the firm set of her jaw and the lines between her gathered brows said she fully believed what she was saying. He wanted to put his arms around her and assure her that she was loved, but he couldn't.

He was the last person she'd want holding her. After all, in her book he was lower than pond scum. What was lower than that?

"I don't want to talk anymore about my father. I'd rather think about the beautiful day we had. Maybe it doesn't have to end yet."

Lucas consulted his watch. "Actually, it's almost time for you to head over to see Molly."

It was for the best. He'd already scrapped his plans for this evening—or any evening for that matter. Kate would hate him when she found out that he was an absentee father. And he couldn't blame her. He wasn't pleased about the situation either. He just wanted what was best for his daughter—and now it was going to cost him the respect and friendship of someone who'd given him the gumption to get on with life.

Then again, what if Kate never found out about Carrie? What if he left out that part of his past? But could he do that? Could he deny his own daughter?

Absolutely not. He was not a liar. And he was proud to be Carrie's father. He'd just have to find the right time to tell Kate. Somehow there had to be a way to make her understand. But how?

The next morning, Kate awoke with a definite crick in her neck. She rolled her shoulders, trying to ease the discomfort. Maybe working into the wee hours of the night hadn't been her brightest idea. She'd meant only to sit down on the floor to take a break and the next thing she knew it was morning.

But after that earth-moving kiss in the park during the romantic—dare she say it—date, she'd been full of energy...that was until she'd sat down. She yawned and pushed aside the drop cloth she'd ended up using as a makeshift blanket. Getting to her feet, she stretched her sore muscles.

Heavy footsteps sounded in the upstairs hallway. She glanced at the time on her phone. It was far too early for the workers.

"Kate?" Lucas's voice rang out.

"In here." She smoothed her hair with her palms.

Lucas appeared in the doorway with his hands full. "I thought we'd have something a little different this morning. I ran out for some of that flavored coffee you're always going on about and a couple of blueberry muffins."

"Is this a special occasion?"

He handed over a coffee. "No. I just thought a change in routine might do us good."

She gratefully took a long, slow swallow, letting the warm, creamy coffee fill her mouth with the most delicious flavor. That first sip of the day was by far the best. "I definitely approve."

"When you didn't show up for breakfast, I decided to check on you."

Since when had he started worrying about her? Surely she'd misunderstood. But the fact he'd noticed her missing and tracked her down was something she just couldn't ignore.

"I wanted to start work early. I need to get this done on schedule."

Lucas peered around. With his height and broad chest, he seemed to fill up the room. Awareness awakened Kate's sluggish body. The fresh scent of his cologne wafted past her nose and wrapped around her. Did the man have to smell so good?

He moved, visually examining the balled-up drop cloth on the floor and then taking in her rumpled appearance. "Starting early? It looks more like you never made it to bed."

She shrugged, hoping he wouldn't make a big deal of it. "This coffee sure hits the spot."

He continued looking around before turning back to her. "You're working too hard. If you need more help, just tell me."

"I will." But right now she had something else on her mind. "You know, I was thinking that the night of the fund-raiser would be the perfect time to announce the sale of this place."

He stared at her as if she'd sprouted another head. "Why would I do that?"

"I'm obviously missing something. I know

when we discussed it earlier the situation still wasn't clear, but isn't the point of fixing up the house to put it on the market? I mean it isn't like you live here. In fact, you hate being here—"

"I do not." He looked away, studying something on the floor.

"Don't give me that. Every time I turn around, you're running out the door. I get it. This place doesn't hold good memories for you. I have a couple of places like that myself. So why hold on to the house? Let someone else enjoy it."

He ran a hand through his hair, scattering the short strands. "I don't know if I'm ready to make a decision of that magnitude. Lately, I seem to be making one mistake after the other."

"Does that include kissing me?" Kate clamped her lips shut, but it was too late. Her thoughts were out there. Hovering. Waiting.

She should brush aside her careless comment and pretend she was teasing, but she couldn't. She honestly wanted to know how he felt about her.

With every bit of willpower, she lifted her chin and looked at him. Wondering. Hoping.

His Adam's apple bobbed. Their gazes met. And the air around them seemed to crackle with awareness.

"Kissing you is all I've thought about." His voice was deep and thick, sending goose bumps of excitement down her spine. "My only regret is that it ended far too soon."

His intense gaze held hers. She should turn away. She should… She should…

Long suppressed desires swelled inside her and squelched her train of thought. He stepped forward, closing the gap between them. Her stomach fluttered and dipped. The tip of her tongue swished over her now dry lips. He was going to kiss her again, and she wanted him to because for better or worse, she wanted to taste him on her lips.

The breath in her lungs hitched. She'd never anticipated anything this much in her entire life. Her chin tilted upward. And her heart pounded.

Being cautious wasn't all it was cracked up to be. This once she wanted to throw caution to the wind. She wanted to live in the moment.

She shifted her weight to her tiptoes. And then he was there. His warm breath tickled her cheek before his lips pressed to hers. They moved gently at first, tentatively as though questioning her. But that wasn't nearly enough for her. She met his kiss with a hunger that startled her. He tasted like rich, dark coffee and she'd never tasted anything so good.

Mr. Oh-So-Sexy could most certainly kiss. In fact, she'd never enjoyed anything so much in her life. Her needy body leaned into his hard contours. The fact that he wanted her was all too evident and had her insides melting into a liquid pool of desire.

Standing there, wrapped in his arms, her problems and responsibilities temporarily fell away. In that moment, she was the woman desired by the most thoughtful man she'd ever known, who could kiss the common sense from her mind. But one thought came to mind—one very clear and concise thought.

She was in love with Lucas.

She didn't know where or when it had started, but she was falling hard and fast for him. And try as she might, she couldn't stop her heart from spiraling out of control.

Her fingers blindly plucked at his silk tie, pulling it loose. She fumbled with his shirt buttons until enough were undone that her hands could slip over the bare skin of his shoulders and back. Her core temperature climbed with each tantalizing move.

"Tell me now if you want me to go." His voice was raspy as his fingers slipped beneath her shirt.

"Stay. Please."

Her eyes opened for a second, glancing over to the tangle of drop cloths she'd used not so long ago as a makeshift bed. Not exactly the Plaza Hotel, but right now, it didn't matter. His tongue swept inside her mouth, teasing and taunting. Her thoughts scattered.

They stumbled backward, still clinging to each other. Now that she'd found him, she never wanted to let go. She couldn't get enough of him…of his touch. Lucas lowered them to the floor and they landed with a bit of an "oomph" that jarred their lips from each other.

He brushed a few strands of hair from her face. "Sorry about that."

"It's okay. I had a soft landing."

She was half sitting, half lying in his lap while staring into his darkening eyes. They mesmerized her with their ability to change color with his moods. Right now, she was drowning in them.

She was the first to make the move this time. Hungry for more of him, she leaned forward. Her mouth claimed his—needy and anxious. There was no mistaking the passion in his kiss as he followed her lead.

But then he pulled back just enough to start a trail of kisses down over the sensitive skin of her neck. A moan of desire swelled in her throat. She'd never felt such desire by a man. He gave as good as he got and she couldn't wait to find out what else he was good at.…

CHAPTER THIRTEEN

THE THUD OF work boots on the steps roused Kate as she savored the way her body still thrummed with utter satisfaction. She lifted her cheek from Lucas's bare shoulder. "Shoot. It's Charlie."

Adrenaline pumped through her veins as she scrambled to grab the edge of the white drop cloth. What had she been thinking to do this here?

Obviously her brain had short-circuited as soon as Lucas's lips had touched hers. Now she didn't know how she'd be able to face the foreman. She pressed her hands to her heated cheeks before combing her fingers through her flyaway hair. One look and Charlie would know what had happened. Soon everyone would know. How in the world would these men ever respect her when they found out she was sharing a bed with the owner?

Lucas jumped to his feet, springing over to the door, pushing it shut. Kate didn't need an invitation. She rushed to locate her discarded clothes.

A knock sounded. "Kate, are you in there?"

She held her breath, hoping Lucas had remembered to catch the lock. The doorknob jiggled. When the door didn't budge, she expelled a pent-up breath. But she still felt the heat on her chest rise up her neck and engulf her entire face.

Lucas was the first to find his voice. "She'll be with you in a couple of minutes."

"Mr. Carrington, is that you?"

"Yes. We are going over some plans."

Is that what he called it? If she'd recalled correctly they'd gone over those "plans" a couple of times…at least she had. A fresh wave of heat rolled over her. She didn't even want to know what was going through Charlie's mind. His imagination was probably painting him a pretty accurate picture of their "meeting."

In a flourish of activity, they dressed. Resigned to the fact she'd done her best to fix herself up without a mirror, she turned to Lucas. She straightened his tie and in turn, he ran his fingers through her hair and tucked a few strands behind her ears.

"Ready?" he whispered.

She wasn't, but she had this feeling Charlie wasn't going anywhere. She nodded and Lucas opened the door.

The foreman ducked his gray head inside. His intense stare took in her not-so-neat appearance, before zeroing in on the scattered drop cloth on the floor next to Lucas's rumpled-up suit jacket.

The man's gaze came back to Kate. "Anything you need?"

She shook her head, not trusting her voice. It took all of her determination to keep from wringing her hands together. She'd never been caught in such a compromising situation. She felt like a teenager, experiencing love for the first time.

A knowing smile pulled at the older man's unshaven face. "Sorry. I didn't know you two were... umm, having a private meeting." He winked. "No biggie. We can go over the discrepancy with the paint order later."

Kate was so hot now that beads of moisture dotted her forehead. She swallowed hard and refused to let on that this thing, this moment of craziness with Lucas, had affected her. There would be time to sort things out later...much later. First, she had to get her head wrapped around what had happened.

She stepped toward the door. "Charlie, we can go downstairs and go over it now."

"Nah." He waved her off. "You two finish your umm...meeting. I'll go head off the men so they don't disturb you." He started to turn away, then glanced back. "Ya know, the missus was just showing me the picture of you two in the paper this morning. I told her it wasn't any of our business. But thought you should know."

"Thanks." Lucas didn't smile.

Charlie nodded and pulled the door shut. Neither said a word as the foreman whistled a merry tune as he moved down the hallway.

When they were alone again, Kate groaned. "This is awful. I don't know how I missed hearing his approach. The man's footsteps are louder than a stampede of cattle."

"You weren't the only one who was caught off guard. Did you see the unhappy look on his face when he first walked in? I thought for sure I was going to have to defend myself. Looks like you've won him over."

"We're friends. When you work seven days a week with a person, you get to know a lot about them and their family. Just like you and I have gotten to know each other really well. I don't think he'll say anything."

"It won't matter if he does. The whole city thinks we've been doing this all along."

Lucas adjusted his shirtsleeves before slipping on his suit jacket that now had distinct wrinkles. He kept his head lowered as though it took every bit of his concentration to adjust his clothing. But Kate knew differently—knew he had something else weighing on his mind. He was probably just as confused as she was about where they went from here.

No matter what, she couldn't deny that she'd never been kissed quite so thoroughly in her entire life. Nor touched so tenderly and made to feel that her happiness came first. Lucas was a unique man and his ex-wife must have had a few marbles loose to let him slip away. But she couldn't go losing her head over him. She had to keep her focus on Molly and the fund-raiser.

Lucas looked down at the mess of throws on the floor. "I'll just give you a hand straightening up—"

"No. Don't. I've got it."

"Are you sure?"

"Positive."

She licked her dry lips, noticing how they burned a bit. She couldn't remember the last time they'd been kissed raw. But this day—this beautiful day—she wouldn't forget.

With her back to him, she started to fold the cloth. "Besides, I have to hurry. I need to get to the hospital for an update with Molly's doctor."

Lucas slowly moved to the door before turning back. "At least let me give you a lift."

"This," her hand waved around, unsure how to label what had just happened between them, "doesn't change anything. I have a sick daughter and that has to be my focus. Not you and me.

Not this moment when we both lost our heads. Just Molly."

His mouth opened as though he wanted to say something, then closed.

When he didn't leave, she added, "As for getting to the hospital, I'll be fine on my own. Always have been. Always will be."

"I never doubted it." There was a strained pause. "But will you have enough time to get cleaned up and walk to the hospital?"

She glanced down at her wrinkled work clothes. Drat. She hated that he'd made a valid point at her expense. "I...I can grab a cab."

"Listen, I'm sorry about what just happened." Another poignant pause filled the air as she piled the drop cloths in the corner to deal with later. "I lost my head. It won't happen again. You have my word."

He was apologizing? She hadn't seen that one coming. Had their lovemaking been that bad? Was she that out of practice?

Impossible. She knew when a man was into the moment. And Lucas had certainly been into her. So why the regret?

Maybe it had something to do with the ghosts that lurked within these walls? Or more likely he realized that she wouldn't fit into his posh world. She was a nobody from Pennsylvania, who didn't even have enough money to cover her daughter's medical bills.

Certain that she'd be best off keeping as much distance from him as possible, she said, "I've got to go. I'll see you at dinner for your daily update."

Her vision blurred as she walked away. She blinked repeatedly. She'd let herself get caught up in the moment. That had been her mistake. One she didn't intend to repeat—no matter how much her heart said otherwise.

She dashed the moisture from her lashes. Now how were they supposed to continue with their arrangement? Was it possible to move past something this big—this memorable?

Lucas hated that he'd lost control. He'd been a grump all day to the point of scaring his administrative assistant with a snarly response. He'd of course apologized, but she still kept her distance the rest of the day.

Unable to concentrate at the office, he'd come home earlier than normal. He sat at the kitchen table for a long time, staring blindly at the blinking cursor on his computer. His thoughts kept replaying how he'd made love to Kate. What he'd thought would be a chance to scratch an itch had turned into a mind-blowing moment.

From the second he'd laid eyes on Kate that morning, he'd been a goner. With her hair all tousled and her cheeks rosy, she was a natural beauty. There was nothing phony and artificial about her. He couldn't help but imagine what it'd be like to wake up next to her each morning. That had been his first mistake.

He'd only compounded matters with his second mistake, kissing her. And though he'd savored every delicious moment of their lovemaking—a memory he wasn't likely to forget anytime soon— he couldn't repeat it. For both of their sakes. Once she found out about Carrie, she'd never look at him the same way.

With difficulty, Lucas choked down that last thought. If only there was some way of convincing her that sometimes people made choices they wouldn't normally make in order to spare those they loved.

Lucas's fingers moved over the keyboard, examining the social media campaign planned for the upcoming jewelry launch—Fiery Hearts. He wanted the name on every social media outlet. He was monitoring the Fiery Hearts campaign very closely. Nothing could go wrong.

He didn't really understand the allure of these social sites. He avoided them like the plague. But he was all for different strokes for different folks. And as a businessman, these places were invaluable resources for interactive advertising and research.

He opened a window for MyFriends, keyed in his name and pulled up his personal account that he used to help get the word out about Carrington promotions. He was surprised to find that even with infrequent postings, he'd gained a number of friends.

He moved to the Carrington Gems MyFriends page, which he was pleased to find had a larger following than the last report he'd received. He read over the last few postings, happy to find excitement growing over the launch.

Once he shared the information about the Fiery Hearts reveal from the Carrington Gems page on his personal page, he also decided to share the announcement about Kate's fund-raiser. The posting included a photo of Kate and her daughter. They certainly looked a lot alike—both beautiful. He smiled.

With his work done on the site, he wondered if Kate had an account. It would be one way to keep in contact with her when this fund-raiser was over and she moved on. For her, he just might become more active on social media. He searched for her name but didn't turn up any results. Then for curiosity's sake, he typed his mother's name and when her face appeared on the screen, his mouth gaped. It seemed MyFriends must be a trendy hotspot.

Then on a lark he typed in Floyd Whitley. Immediately he got a listing. There were three candidates. Lucas knew that he should stop there. But what would it hurt to do a little more digging?

He quickly narrowed the list by nationality and he had one candidate. And Kate resembled the man with her dark hair and her big brown eyes. What were the chances this wasn't her father?

But the man's details were hidden because they weren't friends. So Lucas hit the "Be MyFriend" button. As the message sent, Lucas wondered about Floyd's reason for leaving his little girl. No matter what Kate thought, most people just didn't walk away without a reason.

And then without warning a message popped up on his screen. Floyd had accepted his invitation. Now what? Common sense said he should back away. But when a message appeared on the screen, Lucas was drawn in.

Floyd: Do I know you?

What had Lucas been thinking to contact this man? Had he lost his mind? He didn't have any right to be interfering in Kate's private life just to try and make himself look better in her eyes. For all he knew this man could be nothing but trouble.

"Whatcha doing?" Kate came in the back door.

Lucas slammed his laptop closed. If Kate ever found out he'd opened Pandora's box, she would never forgive him. And he couldn't blame her. He'd let his curiosity get out of hand.

"I...I was just doing some work."

"You look like things aren't going well."

He got up, filled his coffee cup to the top and stared at the rising steam. Shoving aside his near misstep with Floyd, he knew there was something much more important he needed to do—tell Kate about his daughter.

Maybe if he'd done this sooner, he wouldn't have gotten the crazy idea to hunt down her father. He wouldn't have gone off on a lark to prove to her that there are legitimate reasons people walk away from their children.

Lucas turned, finding her still smiling at him. "What has you so happy?"

"I talked to your aunt last night and she said since the second photo appeared in the paper, ticket sales have increased to the point where she thinks we'll sell out. You don't know what a relief that is, but of course, your aunt is insisting we keep up the pretense of being a happy couple until the event. Will that be a problem?"

He shook his head. "Not for me."

"By the way, Molly's excited about the idea of vacationing right here in the Big Apple."

"That's great." He was happy to know that he'd done at least that much right.

As the silence dragged on, Kate sent him a

quizzical look. "You know, I was showing Molly the pictures of the carriage and the carousel and she got excited. Except she said when we go for a ride, she wants to pet the horses. Do you think that'll be a problem?"

Lucas shook his head. "Shouldn't be."

Before he could say more, Kate rushed on. "And she made me promise to take pictures of some huge toy store. I don't know how she heard about it, but she wants pictures of the giant piano. So since you're good at playing tour director, what do you say? Want to go with me this week?"

What did he say now? He couldn't refuse Kate anything. Not when she looked at him with those hopeful eyes.

"We'll go," he mumbled.

"You promise? I don't want to let Molly down. So if you aren't up for it, I'll go by myself."

"I promise." He stiffened his shoulders and swallowed. He couldn't drag this out any longer. The truth had to come out now. "I have something to tell you."

CHAPTER FOURTEEN

THE HAIRS ON Kate's arms rose. Something was wrong. Tension rippled off Lucas in waves. And no matter how much she tried to sidestep it with a smile and light conversation, he wouldn't let go of whatever was bothering him. It must be something pretty big.

He stepped closer. "I don't know how to say this."

Say what? Had he changed his mind about having the party here? Surely that couldn't be it. There was no way they could change venues at this late date. The party was only a couple of weeks away.

"Whatever it is we'll work it out."

"I wish it was that easy. The thing is—"

"Excuse me." One of the men Lucas had hired to lighten her workload entered the kitchen. He looked a bit uncomfortable and stuffed his hands in his pants pockets. "Ms. Whitley, we're having a problem. You know that room you wanted us to empty? Well, we're having a problem fitting everything into that smaller room."

"It'll fit. There wasn't that much furniture to move."

"That's the thing—it's not the furniture. It's all of the toys and stuffed animals."

"Toys?" The whole time she'd been working here, she hadn't seen any child's items. None at all. Her gaze sought out Lucas. "Do you know what he's talking about?"

"Damn." Lucas's mug slammed down on the counter, causing Kate to jump.

He moved with long, swift strides as if the house was on fire. She practically had to run to keep up with him. What in the world was going on? Toys? In this place?

Once they made it to the top of the staircase, Lucas turned left instead of right. Suddenly things started to make sense. When she'd told James to clear out the room at the end of the hall, he must have gotten her instructions mixed up and gone to the wrong end—the room with the locked door.

Lucas's shoulders were rigid and his hands clenched. The angry vibes reverberated down the hallway. He'd agreed to the fund-raiser under one condition—that this room not be disturbed. How in the world was she going to make him understand it was an accident?

Lucas came to a stop in the open doorway. "Where are the pictures? The crib?"

"We moved them into the spare room down the hall. One of the rooms that doesn't have any damage like Ms. Whitley told us."

"And did she also tell you to break the lock on the door?"

The man's face paled and he shook his head. "We thought the doorknob was jammed. So we removed the handle. Sorry 'bout that."

"Go. Now." Lucas turned his back on the man.

The workman sent Kate an uncertain look. She waved him away. But Lucas had another thing coming if he thought she could be dismissed so easily. Especially when she didn't have a clue what was going on here.

Lucas's large frame practically filled the doorway. She had to peer around him to get a glimpse into the room. It was painted pink with white-and-yellow flowers stenciled about the white chair rail. There was a gigantic stuffed polar bear with a great big red bow. And a wooden rocking horse. This was definitely a baby girl's room.

Before Kate could formulate any questions, Lucas turned an accusative stare her way. "We had an agreement. You promised not to bother this room."

"I didn't. I swear."

Kate pressed her hands into her hips and pulled

her shoulders back. She wasn't about to take the blame for a mistake that obviously wasn't hers. Surely Lucas had to understand that sometimes misunderstandings happened.

He raked his fingers through his hair, scattering the short strands. "I never should have agreed to any of this."

Her curious gaze returned to the nursery. This stuff wasn't old. It was actually quite modern and very expensive, which meant that up until recently there had been a child here.

She turned on Lucas. "Is this your daughter's room?"

Lines etched his face, aging him about ten years. "Yes. Her name's Carrie."

This news shocked Kate. After she'd opened up to him about so much of her life, including the ugly stuff she didn't share with anyone, she felt as if their friendship was one-sided.

"Why is this the first I'm hearing of her?"

"What do you want to know?"

"Everything. Who is she? Where is she?" Then a horrible thought struck her. Was it possible something had happened to his daughter? Was that why he'd reacted so strangely in the pediatric ward? "Did...did she die?"

"No." A moment passed before Lucas spoke up. "Carrie is a healthy, active four-year-old."

"But I don't understand. This room is made up for a baby. Where is she?"

He ran his hand over his face. "I changed my mind. I don't want to talk about her."

That answer wasn't good enough, not after he'd pressed her to dredge up the information about Floyd.

"Obviously you've been keeping this to yourself for far too long. Look at this house. You've kept it locked up like some museum. I'm guessing you did this to hold in all of the memories. If you won't talk to me, you should find someone to talk to."

"Fine." He exhaled a long, weary sigh. "If you want to know the truth, my ex-wife left me and took our daughter."

Kate knew she was missing a piece of the puzzle because she couldn't make sense of his anguish, his need to keep this room locked up. "You must miss her terribly."

"More than you know…"

Kate approached him and reached out, touching his arm. "I'm sure when you have her here for visitation, she sees how much you love her. She won't forget you. You're her daddy."

He jerked away from her touch. "Carrie doesn't know me."

Surely she hadn't heard him correctly. "What do you mean she doesn't know you?"

"I mean she lives in California with her mother."

"And?"

"There's no and. That's it. End of story. They have their life and I have mine."

The jagged pieces of this puzzle fell into place. She knew this picture—had lived out a similar experience. Lucas was just like her father, a love 'em and leave 'em type. And like a fool, she'd gone and opened her heart to him.

Anger, frustration and disillusionment bubbled up in her. "You don't see your own child? But why? How can you just forget her, like she never existed?"

He nailed her with a stern look. "I will never forget her. Ever!"

"Then why isn't she here with you? At least part-time?"

"It's better this way."

"Better for whom? You?"

"Of course not. Do you think I like this?" His shoulders drooped and his gaze no longer met hers. "Do you think I enjoy having my daughter run from me because I'm a stranger to her?"

Kate crossed her arms and angled her chin. "It doesn't have to be that way."

He shook his head. "You don't understand."

"Then explain it to me."

He sighed. "My ex-wife has gone to great lengths to keep me from my daughter. And now that she's remarried, she doesn't want me ruining her picture-perfect family. She's threatened to make everyone's life impossible if I push her on this."

"She can't just keep you from seeing your daughter because it suits her. You have rights—"

"And I also know what it's like to be the pawn between two warring parents—how torn you feel when they want you to take sides. If it wasn't for Aunt Connie looking out for me, I don't know what I'd have done to get away from the fighting." A muscle twitched in his jaw as he stared off into space. "I won't put my daughter through that."

"So instead you'll let your daughter wonder the rest of her life why you didn't love her enough to stick around." Kate's voice wobbled. "You ran instead of standing up and doing the right thing for your daughter."

"I'm doing what's best for Carrie—"

"No. You did what was best for you." Her chest ached as though her heart had been ripped out. "You aren't the man I thought you were."

His head lowered. "I suppose I'm not."

"How could you keep this all a secret after I opened up to you about my father? I started to think we might have a future. I was so wrong."

"And I was wrong to let you in this house. You need to leave." He strode away, leaving her to make sense of things.

"What? But the fund-raiser—"

"Can be held elsewhere. I don't care where you hold it as long as it isn't here. I don't want anything else moved or disturbed. Send those men away."

Lucas stormed off down the hallway. He couldn't be serious. After all the work, all the plans, he was canceling everything? The backs of Kate's eyes stung. She blinked repeatedly. One lousy mistake and her chance to raise the money for her daughter went up in a puff of smoke. She told herself that's what the tears were about—not the fact that Lucas had been keeping this big secret from her.

She swiped her cheeks and sucked in a shaky breath. Things couldn't end like this. He had to be reasonable about the party. They had an agreement. She started after him.

By the time she made it downstairs, Lucas was gone. There was only one thing for her to do. Leave. But this wasn't over. Not by a long shot. But first they both needed to cool down.

Lucas stood alone in the elevator. Just him and a fuzzy pink teddy bear that was wearing a pink rhinestone tiara he'd had specially made for Molly. He hadn't seen or heard from Kate since he'd reacted without thinking and fired everyone. And he couldn't just leave things like this. He wouldn't let Kate or her daughter down. He had to do something to remedy things. Something drastic.

He stared down at the wide-eyed stuffed animal and started to think over what Kate had said the other day about Carrie. Was Kate right? Would his daughter believe he didn't love her? Surely when she was older she'd understand his reasoning. Wouldn't she?

He pushed aside the thoughts of his daughter, though they were never far from reach. But for these next few moments, he needed to be focused.

"This will all work out." When he realized he was talking to a teddy bear, he moved the stuffed animal behind his back.

The elevator door slid open and Lucas took a deep, steadying breath. A painted giraffe and smiling rhino greeted him, but he didn't smile back. Hesitantly putting one foot in front of the other, he started down the long hallway. The sounds of young children echoed between the walls. The voices still dug and poked at his scarred heart, but he refused to turn around. This trip was more important than his own pain and guilt.

On the ride here, he'd debated how to say what needed to be said. He still didn't have a plan. That in and of itself was so unlike him. He was a visionary. He knew where he wanted his business to go and he took the lead. This time he didn't have a clear vision, only the hope that there was some happy solution to this mess.

He paused outside Room 529. The lilt of Kate's voice followed by a giggle filled the air. He took a deep breath and then rapped his knuckles on the propped-open door before stepping inside the dimly lit room.

"Who's that?" The little girl, who was the spitting image of Kate, pointed at him.

Surprise lit up Kate's face. "Well, that's…umm, was—"

"I'm your mommy's friend. You can call me Lucas."

Molly's gaze swung between him and her mother as though trying to make up her mind whether to like him or not. At last, she smiled. "What's behind your back?"

"Who, me? I don't have anything behind me." He turned around in a circle as though to look behind him, all the while holding the pink bear against his back. "See. I told you there was nothing there."

Molly giggled and Kate smiled.

"Silly, it's right there. Behind you."

Once again he turned around. "I'm telling you, I don't see a thing. Maybe they should check your eyes while you're here."

"I saw it. It's a pink bear."

"You saw a pink bear?" Molly nodded and he

stepped closer. "Maybe you better point out this bear that's following me around."

He turned slowly this time and just as he predicted, Molly grabbed the bear. "See, here it is. And it has a crown." Molly pulled the tiara off the bear's head and put it on her own. "Lookie, I'm a princess."

"A very pretty one. Just like your mother." Molly giggled and Kate blushed. "You better keep a close eye on that bear. He seems to like getting himself into mischief."

He winked at Kate and noticed how she fought back a smile. She wasn't as easy to win over as Molly. Oh, well, he'd dug his hole and now it was time for him to pull himself out. But if the gleam in her eyes was any indication, he was making progress, even if she wouldn't admit it.

"I hear you liked the pictures your mother took of the horse and carriage and the merry-go-round."

Molly nodded. "I get to ride them as soon as I get outta here."

"Not quite," Kate corrected. "We have to wait for the doctor to say it's okay."

"And I wanna go play on a giant piano. Have you seen it?"

He really liked this pint-size version of Kate. "I haven't. But it sounds exciting."

"Mommy's going to take me pictures."

"She is?" He glanced over at Kate, hoping to see her stern expression lighten into a smile. No such luck. "Maybe she needs help finding it."

Molly's eyes widened. "You know where it is?"

He nodded. Molly chattered some more before she faded off to sleep while watching a cartoon. Since it was the end of visiting hours, Kate left with him.

When they reached the elevator, Lucas broke the silence. "I'll give you a ride."

Kate's brows lifted. "You don't even know where I'm staying."

"At my place."

She made an indignant sound. "As I recall, I am no longer welcome there."

The elevator door opened and they stepped inside with an older woman and her husband. Kate moved toward the back and he followed.

He leaned near her ear. "I didn't mean for you to actually leave for good. I lost my cool."

Kate's brown eyes flared. "If that's your attempt at an apology, you have a lot to learn."

"Come on, Kate. Surely you've overreacted before and done something without thinking."

She crossed her arms and gazed straight ahead as though he wasn't there.

The older woman turned to him. "Sonny, you need to say you're sorry and buy her some flowers. Women always like that."

Her husband gently elbowed her. "Helen, let the kids work this out on their own."

"I was just trying to help." The elevator stopped and the couple got off.

Alone at last, Lucas moved to stand in front of Kate. "I'm sorry. I shouldn't have said what I did. And I'll buy you a whole flower shop if it'll make you happy again."

"You should know that I have a brown thumb." Her eyes met his. "As for the rest, you're right. You shouldn't have said those things."

The fact she was able to joke around a little about her brown thumb had to be a good sign. "Please, will you come back and finish the project?"

Kate shrugged. "I'll have to think about it."

"Will you at least come back to the house with me?"

"Seeing as my things are still there, I suppose."

Boy, she wasn't going to make it easy. Then again, he hadn't exactly been easy to deal with either the other day. He could only hope that with time she'd give him a second chance.

CHAPTER FIFTEEN

IT CERTAINLY WASN'T easy. Not at all.

But over the course of the following week, Lucas had convinced Kate he was truly sorry for his outburst. In the end, Kate agreed it was best for everyone to go ahead with the fund-raiser. In return, he insisted on keeping his promise to escort her to New York's grandest toy store. He cajoled her into allowing him to buy Molly a dolly with a few accessories. After all, what was a doll without a wardrobe? Even guys like him knew how important clothes were to both big and little girls.

With only a week to go before the sold-out Roaring Twenties fund-raiser, Lucas was surprised by how well things were progressing with the house. Of course, circumstances could still be better between him and Kate. He planned to work on that, starting with a fancy dinner out.

He was just about to ask her out when her phone rang. As she talked to the unknown caller, her happy face morphed into one of an angry mother bear. "Yes…I understand…I'll be there."

He'd never seen her look so cross. His foot tapped the floor as he waited for the phone call to end. "Is Molly all right?"

"Physically she's fine. Emotionally, that's another story. That was Judy, one of Molly's nurses. She called to let me know Chad was just there to say goodbye."

"But how can he leave now? Molly's surgery is next week."

Kate's hands tensed. "He got a business offer in Tucson. Too good to pass up. He'll supposedly be back as soon as he can."

Lucas watched as Kate paced. He wanted to comfort her, to put his arms around her and pull her close, but he wasn't sure that's what she'd want. Reading women was not something he excelled at. So he sat at the counter, waiting and watching.

"This is classic Chad behavior. Worry about himself first. And the hell with everyone else." She paced back and forth. "This is my fault. My gut said he wouldn't stick it out, but I let him get close to Molly anyway. When will I learn not to count on people to hang around?"

An urge came over Lucas to say she could count on him. He wouldn't walk away. The thought caught him off guard. Was that truly how he felt? Or was he merely sympathizing with her?

She stopped and faced Lucas, her eyes round like quarters. "The house. The men. What am I going to do? Molly needs me. The nurse said she was in tears. But there are still things to do here before the party. I…I…"

He appreciated that Kate took her obligations so seriously. Maybe that was his problem—he took his work way too seriously. It'd cost him dearly. He didn't want Kate to make the same mistakes—putting work ahead of family.

But that would mean he'd have to step up and take over the house renovations. When he'd first met Kate, he'd have never dreamed of working upstairs amongst the memories, but now…

He might not be ready to pledge to Kate forever, but this burden with the house, this was something that he could do for her. It was a chance to show her that not all men were like her father and her ex-husband. He wouldn't cut and run when times got tough. He would be her friend as long as she wanted.

Firm in his decisions, he reached for his keys. "Here. Take the car. And don't worry about things here."

"But it's not finished. The paintings and furniture still need to be placed. And the nursery.

I never got a chance to put it back together. I'm sorry." Her eyes filled with tears.

Lucas pulled her close. He rubbed her back while resting his head against hers. "Don't worry. Between Charlie and me, we've got it covered."

Kate pulled away and stared up at him. "But you have your work and the Fiery Hearts launch. And you're already short your marketing director."

"I will take care of everything. I promise. Now go. Be with your daughter. And stop worrying. I've got this under control."

With Kate out the door, Lucas phoned his extremely organized assistant. For the first time in almost two years, he told her he would be out of the office. He relayed what needed to be done in terms of the San Francisco project and the launch of the new jewelry line. He also told her that if she needed him, he'd be at home for the next week—words he'd never said to her at such a critical juncture for Carrington Gems. And he knew he'd made the right choice.

Not so long ago, he wouldn't have believed it… but sometimes there were things more important than work. Kate was counting on him. And he vowed not to let her down.

Lucas changed into a pair of comfy jeans and a ratty old T-shirt. He moved swiftly back to the kitchen where he'd left some rough sketches Kate had done up for him to show him how she planned to stage each room. They'd be his saving grace, but when he sorted through the pile of papers and receipts to locate the drawings, they weren't nearly as detailed as he'd thought.

"How hard can it be?" he muttered to himself as he moved through the hallway.

Taking a deep breath, he started up the steps. He took them two at a time and paused at the top when he came face-to-face with a portrait of his great-grandparents on the opposite wall. They were the inspiration for the Roaring Twenties party. He hadn't seen this part of his past in years…ever since Elaina had decided the mansion needed a more modern look.

He smiled as his gaze moved down the hallway, taking in the paintings that had hung in this house as far back as he could remember. Kate had thoroughly disagreed with his ex-wife's decor, going with a more traditional look. He thoroughly approved of Kate's approach and the use of family portraits and heirlooms.

He felt more at peace in these rooms than he had in a very long time. The tension in his neck and shoulders eased. Kate had worked miracles to turn this place into a home. And now it was time he worked one of his own.

His gaze paused on the open doorway to the nursery. He could put the room back to the way it had been before the workers dismantled it. He recalled the room down to its finest details. But this room wasn't his priority. He pulled the door shut and locked it. He would deal with it another day. There was something more important he needed to do.

A week had passed and Kate couldn't wait to see Lucas's attempt at remodeling. He'd been keeping her bedroom off-limits until he finished.

"Close your eyes." When she didn't move, he lifted her hand over her eyes. "And no peeking."

She shook her head. "You're worse than a little kid."

"It'll be worth it. I promise."

She did as he said while letting him guide her down the hallway. "Okay, you can open them."

Kate smiled as she stood at the doorway of the original bedroom she'd been using up until Lucas had taken over finishing the upstairs. "Wow. I didn't expect you to do such an amazing job."

"I had a great incentive."

She turned to see him staring directly at her. Her heart fluttered and heat rushed up her neck, flooding her face. Had he really done all this for her?

The once bright white walls were now a soothing sandy tan. And the crown molding had been repaired and painted a soft, creamy white that matched the ceiling. She couldn't have done better if she'd picked the colors herself. The furnishings were new. The dark wood of the big sleigh bed fit perfectly in the room.

"Seems you have a hidden talent. I guess you don't need my services after all."

Lucas's head ducked. "The truth of the matter is I sort of…umm…hired the woman at the furniture store to help me get the details right. I know you were making a point of using the furniture that has been in my family for years, but I wanted something new for this room."

She was impressed Lucas seemed to be moving forward and letting go of his tight grip on the past. She wanted to turn and throw her arms around him, but she held back, waiting to hear his reasoning for the new furniture and the impressive makeover.

Lucas took her by the hand and drew her inside. It was only then that she noticed a small table off to the side, all done up with a lace tablecloth, tapered candles and a long-stem red rose. China and stemware completed the impressive setup. No one had ever done anything so romantic for her.

Kate's mouth gaped. "Is this for us?"

"Unless you were planning to have a late dinner with someone else."

"Definitely not. I just wasn't expecting you to go to all of this trouble."

Lucas shrugged. "I thought you might like it, but if you don't, we could go back downstairs."

"Oh, no, this is fine." She glanced down at her jeans and blue cotton top, feeling severely underdressed. "Maybe I should get changed."

"Not a chance. You look beautiful just like that."

Her stomach fluttered.

"Would you like some champagne?" He moved to the table and withdrew a bottle from an ice bucket and held it out to her.

Her gaze strayed over to the bed where the beige comforter was already drawn back. Her pulse accelerated. Lucas was attempting to seduce her. They hadn't made love since that one time, both agreeing that it would be best for their working relationship to keep things casual. So what had changed? Or was she reading more into this than he intended?

"Lucas, I don't understand."

Her stomach was aflutter with nerves as she waited and wondered where this night was headed. Where did she want it to go?

Lucas walked up to her. "I'm sorry things between us have been so bumpy. I'm hoping they'll be better from now on."

He wrapped his hands around her waist. The heat of his touch radiated through her clothing. Her heart thumped with anticipation. He was trying to show her that he could change and she wanted nothing more than to give him a second chance.

His head dipped and she leaned into him, enjoying the way his mouth moved over hers. Each time their lips met, it was like the first time. And she never wanted it to end. Because with each kiss, her heart took flight and soared.

But she couldn't lose control now. She couldn't cave into the desire warming her veins just yet. First, she needed some answers.

With every bit of willpower she could muster, she braced her hands on his shoulders and pushed away. She drew in an uneven breath and willed her pulse to slow. She glanced up, seeing the confusion in his eyes.

"We need to talk." She took a deep breath, hoping the extra oxygen would help clear her thoughts. "This is beautiful, but why have you gone to all of this trouble?"

Her fevered wish was for him to say he loved her. That he needed her. And that he was ready to make peace with the past and reach for the future she knew they could have together.

"I thought it was self-explanatory."

She licked her dry lips, searching for the right words. "Is this the beginning of something? Will you still be interested in me...in us next week? Next month?"

"I…I don't know. You're rushing things."

Kate shook her head. "I'm not rushing anything. This—" she waved her hand around "—was your idea. Are you saying there's room here for me and Molly in your life?"

His brows lifted. "You mean here, in this house?"

She nodded. Inside she was begging him to pick her, to choose a future with her.

"I don't know if I can live here with another family."

His lack of certainty hurt her deeply. She loved him. She'd accepted that fact back when they'd made love. Even though she'd been fighting it, it'd only grown stronger.

"And does that include your daughter? Do you not have room for her here either?"

"You don't know what you're asking."

"Yes, I do. I'm asking you to show your daughter how much she is loved. To keep her from ending up like me, with no family around for the good times and the bad."

"But what if she gets hurt in the cross fire between her mother and me?"

"You'll see that it doesn't happen."

He moved closer, reaching out to Kate. "None of this has to stand between us."

"You never said what it is you want for us."

His hands lowered to his sides. "Why do you

need it defined? Can't we just take it one day at a time?"

She drew in a breath and leveled her shoulders. "At the beginning, I thought that something casual would be enough. But it isn't. Soon Molly will be getting out of the hospital and she'll be asking questions about you and me. What do I tell her if I don't even know the answers myself?"

Lucas raked his fingers through his hair and moved to the other side of the room. "I don't know if I can make a new start. Commitments haven't exactly worked out for me if you haven't noticed."

"I'm not asking you for a commitment. I'm just asking if you care enough about me to explore a future together. Can you do that?"

Before he could say a word, her phone buzzed. She wanted to ignore it. Lucas's next words were so important, but if it was the hospital, she had to take it. She held up a finger, stemming off his response. She withdrew her phone from her pocket.

After a brief conversation with Nurse Judy, Kate turned to him. "I have to leave."

CHAPTER SIXTEEN

KATE SAT BESIDE Molly's bed and watched her little girl sleep peacefully. The night before, the hospital had called because Molly had woken up from a nightmare, crying inconsolably for her daddy. Inside Kate seethed over the man being so thoughtless about carelessly dropping in and out of his child's life.

At least Lucas didn't put his daughter through that kind of hurt, but he could do so much more. He could be a reliable part of his daughter's life, if he'd get past his worries. Sure, it might not be easy for him to deal with his ex-wife, but she knew how important it was for a child. And she just couldn't be involved with someone who wasn't there for his family through thick and thin.

She watched her daughter take a late-day nap after one of her treatments. In a couple of hours the fund-raiser was due to kick off. She'd been counting on Chad to watch over their daughter while she attended the event and met with donors. Chad hadn't been thrilled about the idea of being left out of the swanky party, as he put it, but she'd pushed how important it was for Molly and he'd grudgingly relented. So much for him being there for them.

"How's she doing?" came a very soft male voice.

Kate jerked around to find Lucas standing just inside the room. His face was drawn and his eyes were bloodshot as though he hadn't gotten any sleep. She hated how she'd had to run out on their conversation the night before. So much had been left unsaid.

"She's doing better." Kate still got angry every time she thought of how Chad had skipped out, leaving Molly disappointed and heartbroken. "I thought you'd be at the house getting ready for the party tonight."

"Between my assistant and Aunt Connie, they have everything under control. What they really need is you."

Kate's gaze strayed to her sleeping daughter. "I can't leave her alone."

"But you are needed for something very important."

The house was complete. The party was under control. She couldn't think of a single thing that needed her attention. "What is it?"

He pulled a black velvet box from behind his

back. "I need you to wear this tonight when you meet your guests."

Excitement pulsed in her veins. "Is this from the Fiery Hearts line?"

"Yes, it is. I know how anxious you've been to get the first glimpse. I only have a few of the pieces, but they are the stars."

"Hurray!" She quietly clapped her hands together in excitement. "Show me."

He flipped open the lid and her mouth dropped open at the heart-shaped ruby and pearl choker with a matching bracelet and earrings. She reached out to trace her finger over them.

"They're gorgeous."

"You approve?"

She nodded, still taking in their beauty. Nurse Judy entered the room to check Molly's vitals.

"Look, Judy." Kate pointed at the sparkling jewelry. "Aren't they gorgeous?"

"They're stunning. Someone sure knows how to pick out great gifts."

"This isn't a gift." Kate shook her head. "These are part of Carrington Gems' newest line."

"Actually," Lucas interrupted, "they are for Kate to wear to the party tonight."

"I couldn't." Kate pressed a hand to her chest, feeling a bit flustered. "You were supposed to have some beautiful model show them off."

He smiled and continued holding the jewelry for her to take. Judy moved over to Molly's bed while Kate tried to figure out what this all meant…if anything.

He gazed deep into her eyes as he pressed the box into her hands. "I can't think of anyone more beautiful than you."

"But…but I can't. I have to stay here."

"This is one party you aren't going to miss. And that's why I'm here. I will sit with Molly."

"You? You're the one who should be at the party. It's your house."

"Ah…but this evening is your creation. And you are the infamous woman in the photo that everyone wants to meet. You will be the star."

She hated that he had a point. This was her party—her idea. The thought that people were going to attend with the interest in meeting her made her stomach quiver.

"And," he added, "I need you to be the face of Carrington Gems."

"Me? I couldn't." She worried her bottom lip. "You need someone beautiful—"

"Someone just like you. And if you need anything my aunt and my assistant will be on hand."

Kate cast a hesitant glance at Molly. She really didn't want to leave her, but this fund-raiser was vital for her surgery. Maybe if she just slipped out for an hour or two…

Judy caught her gaze and smiled. "Go. Molly

will be fine. There are plenty of people around here who will keep an eye on her. And I promise we will call you if anything comes up."

Kate stood, still feeling so unsure about this arrangement. She looked into Lucas's steady blue gaze and could feel his strength grounding her. He placed the jewelry case in her hand.

"There's a car waiting downstairs to whisk you off to the ball."

"Just like Cinderella."

"Most definitely."

If only her Prince Charming was going to meet her at the party. But this wasn't a fairy tale. This was reality. She'd been on her own before—why should tonight be any different?

Lucas settled back in the chair, leafing through the financial magazine he'd brought along. He couldn't remember the last time he'd been able to sit down and read something besides sales reports and marketing projections. He glanced over at Molly as she cuddled with the pink teddy bear in her sleep. She was so cute—so like her mother.

"Okay, you can go."

He glanced up, finding Judy standing there. "Go where?"

"Cinderella needs her Prince Charming. So off to the ball with you."

"I can't. I promised to watch over Molly."

"I just got off duty and my husband said he'd entertain our little ones with a pizza and movie so I have the evening free. I know you're dying to be with Kate. So go."

"Is it that obvious?"

She nodded.

"Do you think Kate will mind? I mean, I don't know how this works."

"Kate has become a friend. It'll be okay. Remember, I am a nurse. Molly will be in good hands." She sent him a reassuring smile.

Lucas prayed that Judy was right. He headed out the door and rushed home, finding the mansion all lit up. It'd been so many years since it'd come to life like this. Instead of the dread he thought he'd feel, he was excited to see Kate. He had something to tell her…something very important.

And what could be better than telling her at the party? It would be a night to remember. Anticipation flooded his veins as he moved with lightning speed through the back door, past the servers dressed in old-fashioned police uniforms. He chuckled to himself at the irony of having police officers serving drinks at a prohibition party. Kate certainly had a sense of humor.

He quickly showered and changed into his tux. By then the party was in full swing. He really didn't want to face the people or the questions. But he had to do this for Kate.

He plastered on a smile and worked his way through the milling guests decked out in 1920s attire from fringe dresses to black pinstripe suits and hats. It was like walking back in time. He smiled and shook hands with people he knew. Some patted him on the back, congratulating him on an excellent party and his choice of such a gorgeous hostess. Lucas promised to stop back later to talk and moved onward.

His gaze searched the crowded living room where a few people were dancing to big-band music. But Kate was nowhere to be seen. He scanned the foyer, followed by the dining room but still no luck. Was it possible she was upstairs showing people around? He started for the steps when he spotted his aunt.

"Do you know where Kate is?"

"Aren't you supposed to be with Molly?"

"Judy got off duty and offered to sit with her so I could be here for Kate. I really need to talk to her, but I haven't been able to catch up with her."

"Finally came to your senses about her, didn't you?"

He nodded. "If she'll give me a chance."

"I think you'll find her showing some interested guests the prohibition tunnel. But Lucas…"

He didn't have time to chat. He'd been waiting

too long for this conversation. Actually, instead of words he intended to show her that he could be the man she needed him to be…the man his family needed him to be.

At last he found her on the landing, talking to an older, familiar gentleman, but Lucas couldn't recall his name. He gazed up at her. A cute black hat was settled over her short bobbed hair. She looked adorable. The Fiery Hearts ruby and pearl choker sparkled on her long neck. His pulse picked up its pace as he imagined replacing the necklace with a string of kisses.

His gaze slid down, taking in every breathtaking detail. In a vintage black dress, her creamy arms were bare except for the matching bracelet. A murmur of approval grew in his throat, but he had enough sense about him to stifle it.

The dropped waist on her dress lent itself to a short skirt, which showed off Kate's long legs in black stockings and black heels. He'd never ever get tired of looking at her. She was by far the most beautiful woman and the ideal choice to wear the Carrington Gems. He gave in to an impulse and let off a long, low whistle.

Kate turned and color tinged her cheeks. He ascended the steps and made a hasty apology to the gentleman before taking her hand and guiding her up the steps.

Kate stopped at the top of the stairs, refusing

to take another step. "Lucas, you're supposed to be at the hospital."

"Judy is sitting with Molly. She said I couldn't miss being here for you and I have something to show you."

He couldn't wait to show her the nursery that he'd changed into a little girl's room—a room for Carrie. If it wasn't for Kate, he might not have understood that letting go of his daughter might hurt her more than fighting to have her in his life. He owed Kate a debt of gratitude.

She withdrew her hand. "Can it wait? I have guests to greet."

"It's important. I've done a lot of thinking about what you said about the future. Just give me a minute to show you what I've come up with."

Her eyes lit up and sparkled with interest. "Since you put it that way, lead the way."

He smiled. This night was going to be unforgettable for both of them. It would be a new beginning full of countless possibilities. His chest filled with a strange sensation—dare it be hope.

"Ms. Whitley." One of the young male servers rushed up the stairs. "Umm…Ms. Whitley." The young man's face filled with color. "I'm sorry to disturb you. I…umm… You're needed downstairs."

She flashed a smile, visibly easing the man's discomfort. "What's the problem?"

"There's a gentleman downstairs. He says he needs to speak with you."

"Please tell him I'll be down in a moment."

The young man shook his head. "He isn't an invited guest. At least I don't think he is. He isn't dressed up. The man says he needs to speak with you right away."

"I'm coming." The young man nodded and hustled back down the stairs while Kate turned to Lucas. "It must be Chad. Seems he came to his senses about leaving. Molly will be so happy. But first I need to have a serious talk with him. Can we finish this later? After the guests leave."

Lucas didn't want to wait. He wanted to show her that he was taking strides to be the man she wanted. But part of that meant having patience—after all, he wasn't going anywhere. Their talk could wait. But that didn't mean he had to like it.

He groaned his impatience and nodded his agreement.

She lifted on her tiptoes and went to press a kiss to his cheek, but he turned his head, catching her lips with his own. He'd never ever tire of kissing her. He went to pull her closer—to deepen the kiss, but she braced her hands on his chest and pushed away. The kiss might have been brief, much too brief, but it promised of more to come.

"Later." She flashed him a teasing smile.

He ran his tongue over his lower lip, savoring

her cherry lip balm. He stifled a groan of frustration. He wanted more of her sweet kisses now… and later. Forever.

The last word caught him off guard. He never thought he'd ever use that seven-letter word in terms of a relationship again. But Kate had come into his black-and-white world and somewhere along the way had added all the colors of the rainbow. His heart was healed and ready to fight for those he loved.

How it'd taken so long for him to come to terms with how he felt about Kate was beyond him. Now, he couldn't wait to tell her that he loved her. He was dying to know if she felt the same way. But what choice did he have but to wait? Only a little longer and then he'd have her the rest of the night.

"Let's go greet your ex."

They'd just turned the landing when Kate asked, "So what was it you wanted to show me—"

Her words hung there as she came to an abrupt halt.

"Kate, are you all right?"

When she didn't move, didn't say anything, he followed her line of vision to an older man with white hair standing at the foot of the stairs. He was definitely too old to be Chad. And there was something vaguely familiar about him. In a pair of jeans and a plaid shirt, he certainly wasn't here for the party. The man stared back at Kate with tears in his eyes.

Panic clutched Lucas's chest. The face. The age. The look. It all came together at once. This was Kate's father—her estranged father, Floyd—the man he'd connected with on MyFriends.

A hush fell over the crowd as though they sensed the tension in the room and were checking it out. The paparazzi covering the event for all of the major news outlets moved in closer. Their flashes lit up the room, causing even more people to move in for a closer view. Lucas waved them off and the flashes stopped. But it was too late— the press was going to have a field day with this story. Guilt weighed heavily on Lucas's shoulders.

Floyd placed a foot on the bottom step and Kate took a step back.

"Katie, you look so beautiful all grown up. You're the spitting image of your mother—"

"Don't! Don't say that. There's nothing you could say that I want to hear. Just go."

"Katie girl, I'm sorry—"

Her voice shook. "I don't know why you picked now to pass through my life, but just keep going. You're good at walking away, so don't let the door hit you on the way out."

Floyd's gaze moved to Lucas. A light of recognition filled the man's eyes.

Lucas might not have talked to the man online,

but looking back now, he realized even seeking him out and sending a friend request had been too much. The man had already been curious about who he was—all he had to do was look on Lucas's MyFriends page to find a picture of Kate. He'd unwittingly laid out a trail of breadcrumbs that anyone could have followed—including Floyd.

Finding his voice, Lucas said, "You should go. Now."

Kate's shocked look turned in Lucas's direction. He froze. The breath trapped in his lungs. He wanted to wind back time and change things, but he couldn't any more than he could ease her pain.

"You did this." Her voice vibrated with emotion. "You brought him here, didn't you?"

Her pointed words jabbed at his heart. He wanted to explain and make her understand that he hadn't invited Floyd here. He'd never ever orchestrate a public reunion.

"I didn't invite him—"

Her eyes narrowed. "But you contacted him, didn't you? You couldn't leave well enough alone."

Lucas wanted to deny it, but he couldn't. He was losing the woman he loved and there wasn't a damned thing he could do about it. He merely nodded.

"You had to prove me wrong, didn't you? You had to prove to me that…that he—" she pointed at Floyd "—had some excuse for leaving me just so you could feel better about walking out on your own daughter. I should have never trusted you. When will I ever learn not to trust people?"

"You can trust me—"

Her chin lifted and her eyes shimmered with unshed tears. "No, I can't. You just proved me right. Molly and I are better off on our own."

Lucas could feel the curious gazes boring into his back. He wasn't worried about himself as he was used to providing fodder for the press, but Kate didn't need her private life made public knowledge.

"Kate, this isn't the place for this."

Her brows drew together. "Maybe you should have thought about that before you started poking around in my life. I'm not the one who made it possible for Floyd to be here. You did that all on your own. I should have known I couldn't trust you. I won't make that mistake again."

Kate spun around and sailed up the stairs. Even though he hadn't invited her father here, he had opened Pandora's box. Like Cinderella running off into the night, Lucas knew their fairy tale had just ended.

CHAPTER SEVENTEEN

IT HAD TO BE HERE. It just had to be.

But search as she might, Lucky Ducky was missing.

Kate shoved aside her purse. How could this happen? Ducky was always in her purse. And as Molly's surgery dragged on, Kate was starting to feel nervous. She knew it was silly, but that toy made her feel somehow connected to Molly. She could still envision her sweet smile when she'd handed over the trinket—back before Molly had gotten sick.

With a sigh, Kate slouched back in the stiff hospital chair. Two days had passed since she'd left Lucas at the party. She still couldn't believe he'd stepped so far over the line by contacting her father. She glanced over at Floyd. He sent her a reassuring smile. It was good to have family around. And if it hadn't been for Lucas's meddling, Floyd wouldn't be here. But did that excuse Lucas's actions?

"You've got plenty of time before we hear anything about the surgery," her father said. "Why don't you call that young man of yours and let him know how things are going?"

"I don't see the point. Even if we find a way to get around what he's done, he'll eventually leave."

"I know you don't have any reason to believe me of all people, but not everyone walks away."

"The people in my life do."

"If he really loves you, like I suspect he does, he'll stick." Her father sighed and ran a hand over his day-old stubble. "Don't let my poor decisions color the rest of your life. If you quit letting people into your life, you'll end up old and alone. You know Molly isn't going to stay small forever. Why don't you give him a call and see what happens?"

She hated to admit it, but Floyd had a point. Molly would eventually move on with her own life. But the thought of putting herself out there only to have Lucas reject her scared her to bits.

"I doubt he'll want to talk to me."

"You'll never know until you try. From the sounds of it, you both have some apologizing to do. But he appears to be a good guy. Is he?"

She nodded. "But I can't forget that he went behind my back and contacted you."

"Everyone makes mistakes." Her father reached over and grasped her hand, giving it a squeeze. "If it wasn't for him, I might never have gotten up my courage to track you down. I know we still have a long ways to go, but you are willing to give me a second chance and what I did was so much worse than Lucas's misstep."

But it was more than Lucas contacting her father—it was the way he was willing to back quietly out of his daughter's life. Sure, he had his reasons, but none of them were good enough to walk away from someone you loved. A lump formed in the back of her throat. But wasn't that what she was about to do—walk away from the man she loved without giving him a chance to explain?

The realization that she still loved Lucas even after everything that had happened jolted her. What should she do now? Ignore her feelings and hope they went away?

"Call Lucas."

It was as if her father was privy to her thoughts. Was that even possible after their extended separation?

Just yesterday morning, the day after the party, Floyd had caught up with her here at the hospital. At first, she hadn't wanted to hear what he had to say, but eventually she reasoned that if she ever majorly messed up with Molly, she'd want to be given a chance to explain.

Her father had struggled with the words, but at last he admitted how he'd gotten caught up in gambling and put the family in deep debt. Things continued downhill to the point where he got involved with some unsavory loan sharks. A shiver had run over her skin when he'd described how they'd roughed him up when he didn't have the money he owed. Unwilling to make his family targets, he'd left. It'd taken him years to conquer his addiction, but by then he figured it was too late to fix things.

"The difference is you were trying to protect us." Though she still hadn't made peace with her father's choices, she was willing to give him a chance as long as he was up-front and honest with her. But there was something she'd wondered about. "Mom never spoke of you after you left. I never understood why."

"I hurt her deeply." Her father leaned back in his seat and ran a hand over his aged face. "Things were so messed up back then. I loved her, but love doesn't mean that two people are good for each other. Your mother and I, we were too different. You and Lucas, do you have things in common?"

She thought of the man who could make her heart skip a beat with just a look. They were different, but not to extremes. They liked the same sorts of food. They both enjoyed quiet evenings at home. And they both thought family was important. Secretly she was missing Lucas and wishing he could be here with her now. When he held her close she felt safe and protected—as if nothing could go wrong.

The push-pull emotions raged inside her. But when it came down to the bottom line, she loved him. Nothing had changed that.

And there was something he'd intended to show her. If she didn't talk to him, she would always wonder what it had been. Would it have made a difference?

Oh, what would it hurt to let him know that thanks to his help, Molly was having her surgery? And she would thank him for bringing her father back into her life. She owed him that much.

"I'm going to step out into the hall." Kate got to her feet. "Can you let me know if there's any news?"

"Sure. Go ahead. I'll be right here."

"You don't know how many years I've waited to hear those words." She started to lean down to kiss his weathered cheek but hesitated. They had a long way to go before they'd be that close. "Thanks."

"Things will be different from here on out. I promise." His voice cracked with emotion. "Now go patch things up with Lucas."

"I'll try." But she wasn't getting her hopes up too high. She already missed Lucas terribly. To set herself up for another fall would be devastating.

* * *

Lucas waited as the hospital elevator stopped at each floor, allowing people to get on and off. Every muscle in his body was tense. Logic said he shouldn't be here. He didn't want to do anything to upset Kate on such an intense day. But he had something important to give her. He stared down at Lucky Ducky in his hand. He ran his thumb over the toy and prayed some of that luck would rub off on him.

His cell phone vibrated and he retrieved it from his pocket. He was surprised to see Kate's name flash across the screen. "Hello."

"Lucas, it's Kate. I…I needed to talk to you."

"Where are you?"

"At the hospital. Today's Molly's surgery."

"Hang on a sec." He worked his way through the throng of people and stepped off the elevator into the hallway. "Any word on how she's doing?"

"Nothing yet. We should hear something soon."

He heard the echo of Kate's voice. He took a few steps and peered down the hallway, finding her leaning against the wall with her back to him. He hesitated, not knowing what sort of greeting to expect. He reconciled himself to the fact that he deserved whatever she dished up.

He continued down the hallway. "Kate, turn around."

When she did, surprise lit up her eyes. She

looked bone-tired and he wanted nothing more than to wrap his arms around her. But he couldn't. It wouldn't be what she wanted after the way things had played out with her father. If only he'd thought it through and realized how easy it'd be for the man to track them down via the party announcement on his MyFriends account.

But it all came down to the fact that he shouldn't have been meddling. He'd totally messed things up. And the only thing he could think to do was apologize and hope she'd forgive him.

They stared at each other, but he was unable to read her thoughts. Her face was devoid of emotion.

"I'm sorry," they said in unison.

"You are?" Again they spoke over each other.

Kate laughed. Her sweet tones washed over him, easing the tension in his neck and shoulders. Maybe there was a chance she didn't hate him. Maybe it wasn't too late to fix things. But he knew he was getting ahead of himself. First things first.

"Kate, I'm sorry about contacting your father. I just thought… Oh, heck, I don't know what I was thinking." He ran a hand over his tense neck. "Maybe I thought if I could show you that your father was a better man than you thought that I'd have a better chance with you."

"You were that serious about me that you

thought you had to go to such lengths to win me over?"

He nodded, fighting back the urge to pull her close and do away with the talking. But something still needed to be said. "Remember how I wanted to show you something at the party?"

She nodded.

"I was wondering how you feel about yellow gingham? At least I think that's what the woman at the store called them—"

"Called what?" Kate's brows drew together as she stared up at him.

"The new curtains I put in the nursery. Well, it isn't a nursery anymore. It's a little girl's room."

Kate's eyes widened. "What are you saying?"

He cleared his throat. "If it wasn't for you, I wouldn't have realized that even though I was working so hard to shield Carrie from seeing her parents fight, she might just be as hurt by the knowledge that I didn't go the extra mile for her. I had a very interesting conversation with my ex-wife's new husband. It seems he's a lot more reasonable since he has kids and an ex-wife. Anyway, he's going to talk to Elaina, and I have my attorney working on a formal visitation schedule. It will be a gradual process until Carrie knows me, but someday I plan to bring her to New York."

"That's wonderful. I'm so happy for you and your daughter."

"And you? Will you be happy, too?"

"That's one of the reasons I was calling you. I wanted to tell you, or I mean, I wanted to thank you for bridging the gap with Floyd. You were right, too. He did have a reason for what he did. As for why he never contacted me later, well, we're working on it."

"Still, I'm sorry I overstepped."

"Is that why you're here? To apologize?"

Then he recalled the trinket in his hand. "Actually, I came to drop off Lucky Ducky. I found him on the floor next to the dresser in your room. I figured today of all days you wouldn't want to be without him."

Kate immediately reached for the keychain and held it close. "Thank you. I was searching for this earlier and I was really upset when I thought I'd lost it. I know it's silly to be so emotional over a cheap toy, but Molly gave it to me and that makes it very special."

And now he had one more important thing to ask her. His gut churned. "I was thinking maybe of starting over and selling the mansion. I'd like to have my new family start in a new home and make new memories." He could see the surprise light up her eyes, but he kept going. He had one chance at getting this right. "Kate, would you consider staying with me and being part of that new future?"

* * *

Had she heard Lucas correctly? He wanted a future with her?

Before her brain had a chance to formulate an answer, her father's voice called out to her. She turned and saw Dr. Hawthorne enter the surgical waiting room. Her heart raced. *Please let it be good news.*

"It's the surgeon. Come on," she called over her shoulder to Lucas.

They rushed down the hallway and joined her father. The surgeon sat down and pulled off his scrub cap. "The surgery was a success."

Tears of joy sprang to Kate's eyes. Her baby had made it. She swiped at her cheeks while Lucas gave her a reassuring smile that made her insides flutter.

The doctor continued going over the results of the surgery. "Lastly you should know that there is no guarantee the tumor won't come back. She'll need to be monitored on a regular basis."

His words rang loud and clear in Kate's mind. A guarantee. That's what she'd been looking for with Lucas. She'd been hoping for the impossible—a man who wouldn't ever fail her. And that was asking the impossible.

Life didn't come with guarantees. You simply had to make the best of the good…and the bad times. A step-by-step process. And she couldn't think of anyone that she wanted to be by her side during that journey more than Lucas.

She reached out to Lucas and slipped her hand in his. His touch was warm and strong. Her heart surged with love.

When her father walked with the surgeon into the hallway, she turned to Lucas and wrapped her arms over his broad shoulders and held on tight. She never wanted to let go.

At last, she'd found what she'd been searching for…her home. It wasn't a building with marble stairs and spacious rooms—it was right here in Lucas's arms…in his heart.

She pulled back just enough to gaze up at him. "I love you."

"I love you, too."

She swiped away more tears of joy. "This has been a day of miracles."

"Does this mean that you'd be willing to face the future together?"

She nodded. "And I think the perfect place to start a whole new life is the Carrington mansion."

"You do? You're not just saying that?"

With her fingertip, she crossed her heart. "I love it and I love you."

EPILOGUE

One year later...

"IT'S GORGEOUS. I don't think there's a single cloud in the sky."

Lucas's gaze never left Kate's face. "Definitely gorgeous."

She glanced over at him and rolled her eyes. "I was talking about this spring day. It's so warm and sunny. Makes me feel like I could conquer anything I set my mind to."

The hum of happy voices filled the air as they stood side by side in Central Park. Lucas smiled. He just couldn't help it. Life was good and he was doing his best to savor every moment.

He wrapped an arm around his wife's shoulders, pulling her close. "You know when I brought you here for the first time, I never dreamed this was possible."

"Well, you better believe it, because those are

our daughters over there petting that horse. Looks like they'll be wanting a carriage ride next."

His mind tripped back in time. "I remember a certain carriage ride and how it earned me a kiss—"

"And a photo in the paper of us in quite a steamy lip-lock."

"I couldn't help myself. I had to see if your kisses were as sweet as I remembered. But they ended up being even sweeter. Want to give it a try now?"

She smiled and shook her head. "Do you have spring fever or something?"

"Just a guy in love with the prettiest girl around."

The past year hadn't been the easiest, not by a long shot. But thanks to Kate, he had opened his eyes and realized that caving in to his ex-wife wasn't in the best interest of their daughter. Carrie was very much a part of him and he felt whole with his family around him. And though it'd been tough at first, he hadn't given up. This was Carrie's first visit to New York and she couldn't have been happier having a sister and another family.

"You seem awfully chipper for a workaholic who has been away from the office all week. Admit it, this staycation isn't so bad."

"Maybe you have a thing or two to teach me after all." He still loved his work, but he'd learned to delegate things when his workload became too heavy. Because he'd found something he loved even more than Carrington Gems—his family.

Kate glanced lovingly up at her husband. How was it possible for him to grow more handsome with each passing day? A smile pulled at her lips.

This past Christmas, they'd had a small ceremony with Molly standing tall by her side. The event had taken place at the Carrington mansion with just a few friends and family invited, including his aunt and her father, who hit it off quite well. It was great having people in their lives to create such precious memories.

Kate's gaze moved from her husband to Molly's glowing face as she ran a hand down the horse's side while her grandfather talked with the horse's owner. "It's hard to believe a year ago Molly was in the hospital. Now, she's a smiling, healthy little girl. I know there's still a possibility that the tumor will return, but with lots of hope and prayers, it's gone for good."

Lucas drew her closer to his side and kissed the top of her head. "Molly is going to have a long, happy life."

"I believe you're right. And now I have one more thing to tell you that will make this day even better."

He gazed down at her. "I don't think that's possible."

She pulled away from him so she could look him in the eyes. "Is that a challenge, Mr. Carrington?"

"Yes, it is, Mrs. Carrington."

She smiled victoriously because she already knew that she'd won. "How would you feel about having a baby?"

The color drained from his face. Not quite the reaction she was expecting. Then his eyes grew round like quarters. And she couldn't be certain, but she'd hazard a guess that he'd stopped breathing.

"Lucas, do you need to sit down?"

"A baby?"

"Yes, a baby. You are happy about this? Aren't you?"

"Woohoo!" He scooped her up in his arms and swung her around in a circle. "We're having a baby!"

His lips pressed to hers. Her heart swelled with love for the most amazing man she'd ever known. Their life might not come with a preordained path, but she knew as long as Lucas was by her side, they'd get through the twists and turns—together.

* * * * *

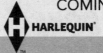

LARGER-PRINT BOOKS!
GET 2 FREE LARGER-PRINT NOVELS PLUS
2 FREE GIFTS!

♦HARLEQUIN®

Romance

From the Heart, For the Heart

YES! Please send me 2 FREE LARGER-PRINT Harlequin® Romance novels and my 2 FREE gifts (gifts are worth about $10). After receiving them, if I don't wish to receive any more books, I can return the shipping statement marked "cancel." If I don't cancel, I will receive 4 brand-new novels every month and be billed just $4.84 per book in the U.S. or $5.24 per book in Canada. That's a savings of at least 19% off the cover price! It's quite a bargain! Shipping and handling is just 50¢ per book in the U.S. and 75¢ per book in Canada.* I understand that accepting the 2 free books and gifts places me under no obligation to buy anything. I can always return a shipment and cancel at any time. Even if I never buy another book, the two free books and gifts are mine to keep forever.

119/319 HDN F43Y

Name	(PLEASE PRINT)

Address	Apt. #

City	State/Prov.	Zip/Postal Code

Signature (if under 18, a parent or guardian must sign)

Mail to the **Harlequin® Reader Service:**
IN U.S.A.: P.O. Box 1867, Buffalo, NY 14240-1867
IN CANADA: P.O. Box 609, Fort Erie, Ontario L2A 5X3
Want to try two free books from another line?
Call 1-800-873-8635 or visit www.ReaderService.com.

* Terms and prices subject to change without notice. Prices do not include applicable taxes. Sales tax applicable in N.Y. Canadian residents will be charged applicable taxes. Offer not valid in Quebec. This offer is limited to one order per household. Not valid for current subscribers to Harlequin Romance Larger-Print books. All orders subject to credit approval. Credit or debit balances in a customer's account(s) may be offset by any other outstanding balance owed by or to the customer. Please allow 4 to 6 weeks for delivery. Offer available while quantities last.

Your Privacy—The Harlequin® Reader Service is committed to protecting your privacy. Our Privacy Policy is available online at www.ReaderService.com or upon request from the Harlequin Reader Service.

We make a portion of our mailing list available to reputable third parties that offer products we believe may interest you. If you prefer that we not exchange your name with third parties, or if you wish to clarify or modify your communication preferences, please visit us at www.ReaderService.com/consumerchoice or write to us at Harlequin Reader Service Preference Service, P.O. Box 9062, Buffalo, NY 14269. Include your complete name and address.

HRLP13R

"SO WISE." HE kissed the back of her hand, the heat of his breath tickling over her skin making her shiver, distracting her for a moment. The old-fashioned gesture was definitely not meant to be shared between employer and nanny. And then he turned her hand over and kissed the palm.

Her breath caught. *Oh, my.*

He regained her attention when he framed her face in two large hands and lifted her gaze to his.

"Thank you." His thumbs feathered over her cheeks collecting the last of her tears. "You are a very giving woman."

"No one should be alone at such a time." She lifted her right hand and wrapped her fingers around one thick wrist, not knowing if she meant to hold him to her or pull him free.

"It's a dangerous trait." The thumb of the hand she held continued to caress her cheek, though he seemed almost unaware of the gesture.

"Why?" she breathed.

"Someone may take advantage of you."

A knot clenched in her gut. Someone had. The harsh memory threatened to destroy the moment. She should step back, return to her duties. But she didn't. Because of the glint of vulnerability in his eyes.

Instead she bit her bottom lip and stayed put. For the first time she successfully shushed it. Perhaps because she needed this moment as much as he did.

"There is only you and me here." She blinked, noting the look in his eyes had changed. The pain lingered but awareness joined the grief. "Are you going to take advantage?"

"Yes." He lowered his head. "I am." And he pressed his mouth to hers. He ran his tongue along the seam of her lips then nipped her bottom lip. "You tempt me so when you torture this lip."

She opened her mouth to protest, but he took full advantage, sealing her mouth with his. Heat bloomed, senses taking over as sensation ignited passion. Large and warm, he dwarfed her, his strong body a shelter against the craziness of the past few days. He drew her closer, aligning her curves with his hard contours and taking the sensual escape to deeper levels.

For long moments she surrendered to his touch, to his heat, to his need. Lifting onto tiptoes she looped her arms around his neck and got lost with him in a world without loss, without hurt, without protocol.

She cleared her throat. "I should check on Sammy."

He nodded and crossed his hands behind his back in a formal pose. To remind himself of duty, or to keep his hands to himself? "I suppose we're going to allocate this to comfort, as well."

"It would be best," she agreed, knowing as she did there'd be even less chance of forgetting these moments in his arms than their last embrace.

Don't miss STOLEN KISS FROM A PRINCE
by Teresa Carpenter, available April 2013!